PUFFIN CLASSICS

TALES FROM
INDIA

BALI RAI has written over thirty books for children and young adults. His first, *(Un)arranged Marriage*, created a huge amount of interest and won many awards, including the Angus Book Award and the Leicester Book of the Year. It was also shortlisted for the prestigious Branford Boase first novel award. *Rani and Sukh* and *The Whisper* were both shortlisted for the Booktrust Teenage Prize. Bali also writes the hugely popular *Soccer Squad* series for younger readers.

Bali was born in Leicester where he still lives, writing full-time and visiting schools to talk about his books. You can visit him at www.balirai.co.uk

Follow Bali Rai on Twitter and Facebook @balirai

BALI RAI

TALES FROM

INDIA

Illustrations by JOE LILLINGTON

PUFFIN BOOKS

UK | USA | Canada | Ireland | Australia
India | New Zealand | South Africa

Puffin Books is part of the Penguin Random House group of companies
whose addresses can be found at global.penguinrandomhouse.com.

www.penguin.co.uk
www.puffin.co.uk
www.ladybird.co.uk

Penguin
Random House
UK

First published 2017
001

Text copyright © Bali Rai, 2017
Illustrations by Joe Lillington
Illustrations copyright © Penguin Books Ltd, 2017

The moral right of the author and illustrator has been asserted

Set in 11.5/15 pt Minion
Typeset by Jouve (UK), Milton Keynes
Printed in Great Britain by Clays Ltd, St Ives plc

A CIP catalogue record for this book is available from the British Library

ISBN: 978—0—141—37306—5

All correspondence to
Puffin Books
Penguin Random House Children's
80 Strand, London WC2R 0RL

*In memory of Karam Singh Dhillon,
as thanks for all the wonderful stories he
shared with me during my childhood*

Also in Puffin Classics

TALES FROM AFRICA
by K. P. Kojo

TALES FROM THE CARIBBEAN
by Trish Cooke

and by Roger Lancelyn Green

TALES OF THE GREEK HEROES
MYTHS OF THE NORSEMEN
TALES OF ANCIENT EGYPT

Contents

AUTHOR'S NOTE

This collection of stories came about after a lunchtime conversation with a friend of mine. It was one of those casual, almost throwaway suggestions that unexpectedly grew into a rather good idea, and one that I was excited to pursue. However, as a British-born child of Indian parents, my knowledge of Indian folk tales was shamefully poor. Of course I knew the famous ones such as the stories of Rama and Sita, but my parents never had the privilege of hearing any such stories because they never went to school. As a result, they had no way of passing these tales on to me.

And in my British schools when I was growing up, the concept of Indian storytelling was almost non-existent. We were never taught about India's rich folk-tale heritage and ancient cultures. Most of us didn't realize that fairy tales and stories of talking animals existed in our parents' cultural backgrounds too. Folk tales, and stories generally, seemed to be a Western thing.

So when the casual idea became a reality, I had to

discover India's rich folk-tale heritage as a beginner. I found amazing and often magical tales, full of adventure and trickery, and infused with deeper messages about morality, life and the world around us. From wicked magicians to wise old priests, charming princes and beautiful princesses – every aspect of the Western tales I'd heard in childhood were present here too.

Perhaps the most surprising aspect was how similar these Indian tales were to those of the Western tradition. Of particular interest were the Indian tales compiled by Joseph Jacobs (1854–1916). These were published in 1912, and form the basis for much of this collection. Punchkin immediately reminded me of Rumpelstiltskin, and many of the animal tales would find a happy home in Aesop or Rudyard Kipling.

Of course, there are many differences too. The Indian tales feel darker in places, and perhaps more moralistic too. Neither do they make allowances for the sensitivity or age of readers. Although a story meant for children, in 'The Peacock and the Crane', the penalty for pride and boastfulness is death, rather than a lesson well learnt. The same goes for any modern concepts of political correctness – there are helpless and passive princesses, and wizened old crones aplenty, not to mention heroes who seem only to relish the acquisition of material wealth. However, this reflects their Western counterparts, so perhaps I shouldn't be too critical.

The rest of the collection comprises retellings of the Akbar and Birbal tales from India's Mughal period, and other gems that I discovered in passing. Better known than most other Indian tales and widely read throughout the country, the Akbar and Birbal stories are wonderfully simple yet leave a lasting impression. Birbal is the patient and wise teacher and Akbar an often impetuous and boastful pupil. Their friendship is warm and full of charm and makes these tales a delight.

In reworking these stories, I will admit to plenty of creative licence. I wanted to make them accessible and readable for Western audiences of all backgrounds. As such, many of the previously published versions needed polishing. Editing stories from *Indian Fairy Tales* by the folklorist Joseph Jacobs was the most challenging and they have seen the greatest changes, although the other tales that I've included have been reimagined too. Keen to keep this collection secular, I have steered clear of religion where possible. I have also removed archaic and often offensive terms, as well as reworking the roles of women in one or two cases.

Continuity and plotting were also an issue. For some of these tales, my starting point was just a few, badly translated lines found online, or in obscure, often self-published books. For others, I had dense passages to work through, most of which lacked clarity. In one case, an entire section seemed to be missing. Where possible,

I stuck to the original plot lines rigidly. For others, this was almost impossible and so I imagined and wrote new connecting scenes. All of this was done to enhance the reading experience and simplify often complicated language.

The aim of this project is to widen the potential readership, and take some of the most popular Indian folk tales to an audience yet to benefit from reading them. Reworking folk tales can be a hazardous business, and often people become attached to their own versions of a particular story. I mean no disrespect by modernizing these tales. Think of them simply as remixes, intended to engage and enchant modern readers, and to lure them further into Indian folklore.

Regardless, I have thoroughly enjoyed compiling these tales. I hope that they give you as much delight as they did me. Happy reading.

Akbar and Birbal Meet

Akbar, third emperor of Mughal India, felt listless. Despite living in a huge palace, surrounded by wealth beyond imagination, he longed for excitement. He tired of jewels and gold, and the finest of foods.

'Majesty, you look so glum. What's the matter?' asked one of his advisors, Abdul Qadir.

'There must be more to life,' Akbar replied.

'I shall summon the jester,' Abdul suggested. 'Or perhaps Your Majesty might prefer musicians and dancers?'

Akbar dismissed all with a wave of his hand. 'Horses!' he eventually ordered. 'Ready my horses. I wish to go hunting.'

Soon, with the sun shining high up above, Akbar and his men galloped through his kingdom, heading for a nearby jungle. Thrilled by the change of scenery, Akbar's spirits soared. His mighty white horse was the fastest in all of India, and the bravest too. The wind cooled his brow as they passed through village after village, cheered on by his subjects.

'A gold coin to the first to bring down a deer!' Akbar cried as they entered the dense jungle. 'A thousand gold coins for a tiger!'

For an hour, Akbar's party toiled deeper and deeper into the trees. Sweat poured from every brow, and soon their horses began to tire. The foliage grew denser still, encroaching from all sides, and they saw no sign of prey. Eventually, exhausted and irritable, Akbar realized that they were lost.

'Which way?' he asked his closest advisors.

'I cannot say, Your Majesty,' replied one.

'We do not know this part of the jungle,' said the next.

'Then what good are you?' the emperor snapped. 'Am I surrounded by imbeciles?'

Dismounting, his men drew their swords and began to hack through the undergrowth, searching for a path of some sort. As Akbar reached for his water gourd, he heard a soft whistling.

'Ssh!' he told his men. 'Do you hear that?'

When none replied, Akbar drew his own sword. 'There is someone here with us,' he whispered.

'Be careful, Majesty – it may be a demon!' warned Abdul.

Akbar, although young, was a wise and rational ruler. He shook his head. Such superstitions were the stuff of children's tales. Demons indeed!

'It's just a man,' Akbar told his men. 'A man who might lead us from this place.'

And true enough, the whistling drew closer and a young man in shabby clothes appeared. In his left hand, he held a ball of string; in his right, a sturdy mahogany staff.

'Your Majesty!' the young man replied, falling to his knees.

'Yes, yes!' Akbar replied. 'Enough of that – who are you?'

The stranger rose and addressed the emperor without eye contact.

'I am just a humble village boy,' the stranger replied. 'My name is Mahesh Das.'

'Well, Mahesh Das, I am Akbar, and I wish to find a way out of this jungle. Can you help us?'

The boy nodded. 'I know this jungle as well as any person can,' he told Akbar. 'It would be an honour to escort you out of here and back to your palace.'

Mahesh held up the ball of string. 'As I walk into the denser parts of the jungle, I tie this string to the trees and bushes . . .'

'To show you the way home . . .' Akbar replied.

'Yes, Your Majesty. The jungle is a living beast. It changes every day.'

The boy turned and followed the string line.

'I shall accompany you on foot,' Akbar told him.

Turning to his men, he pointed to his horse. 'Follow behind,' he ordered. 'And learn from this boy . . .'

As they wound their way back, Akbar and the boy chatted and found that they enjoyed one another's company. Once they reached the gates of the palace, Akbar thanked Mahesh Das and rewarded him with a golden ring. Incredulous and envious, Abdul Qadir seethed.

'But I do not need this,' the boy replied.

'It is a gift,' Akbar told him. 'I insist.'

'Thank you, Majesty.'

'Come to the palace in two days' time,' Akbar told him. 'I wish to offer you a posting at my court.'

Mahesh nodded eagerly, bade his goodbyes, and ran home in excitement. A court role would secure his future.

On the emperor's order, Mahesh returned two days later, only to find a guard barring his way.

'I wish an audience with the emperor,' Mahesh protested.

'Really?' the guard teased. 'Each day a hundred wretched scoundrels beg an audience with His Majesty. What makes you so exceptional?'

Mahesh held out the ring Akbar had given him. 'Here is my pass,' he replied.

The guard considered the ring. A crafty smirk creased his face. Drawing his sword, he ordered Mahesh to follow. In the shadow of a watchtower, he put the blade to Mahesh's throat.

'If he gave you that ring,' the guard said, 'he is sure to give you much more.'

Mahesh, fearing certain death, did not move. His heart pounded against his chest.

'What will prevent me from killing you and taking this expensive ring for myself?'

'N-n-nothing!' gasped Mahesh.

'Let us strike a bargain, then,' the guard told him. 'I will allow you to enter with one condition. I want half of whatever the emperor gives to you. Do you accept – on the life of your mother?'

Mahesh agreed and the guard relaxed his hold.

'Remember well,' the guard warned. 'For if you break your promise, I will kill you!'

Mahesh made his way into court, his mind racing. What could he do but fulfil his bargain, forced though it was? He did not see the disdainful glances from the courtiers, the pained expressions of Akbar's closest advisors, particularly Abdul Qadir. Not even the splendour within the palace took his attention.

'Who are you?' another guard demanded.

'I am Mahesh Das,' the boy replied. 'His Majesty asked me to attend.'

Akbar, on hearing this, called the boy forward, and Mahesh produced his ring.

'Mahesh Das!' the emperor exclaimed with joy. 'You have come!'

'I am here to do your bidding, Majesty,' the boy replied.

Akbar ordered coconut water to be brought for the boy. 'Fruit, sweets?' he added.

Mahesh shook his head but took a little of the water offered. It was cool and sweet, and he savoured it.

'Then tell me, Mahesh Das, what other reward can I give you?'

Mahesh smiled to himself.

'I expect only fifty lashes of the whip, Your Majesty,' he replied. 'Nothing more.'

Akbar was stunned. His courtiers gasped and whispered to one another. Who was this desperate boy? Was he a madman?

'But how can this be?' Akbar asked. 'For what reason do you demand so cruel a reward?'

'Please, Your Majesty,' said Mahesh. 'Allow me to explain after my reward has been received.'

Akbar, proud to be known as a man of his word, nodded sorrowfully. 'So be it,' he whispered. 'Bring the lash.'

As a guard stripped him to the waist and began to administer his reward, Mahesh remained silent. He counted each stroke and upon the twenty-fifth, he asked to speak to Akbar.

'Of course!' the emperor cried. 'Stop at once and send for my physician!'

Mahesh found his breath before revealing all. 'As I entered the palace grounds, the guard accosted me,' he explained. 'He threatened my life and forced on me a pact . . .'

Akbar rose to his feet, his cheeks scarlet with rage. 'FETCH THIS GUARD NOW!' he roared.

'He asked for half of my reward,' Mahesh continued. 'That is why I requested fifty lashes.'

Despite his anger, Akbar found himself smiling. What a sharp and resourceful young man Mahesh Das was! What a wonderful advisor he would make.

'I must ensure your promise is kept, then,' declared Akbar. 'After all, what good is a man whose word cannot be trusted?'

Akbar ordered the guard be given his part of the reward and thrown in jail thereafter. To honour Mahesh, he gave him a new name and position, much to the consternation of his existing advisors. From that day onwards, Mahesh was called Rajah Birbal to signify his cleverness – and he became Akbar's chief minister and friend.

A Most Important Lesson

Akbar was just a boy of thirteen when he became emperor. Surrounded by luxury and revered by his people, he was occasionally guilty of arrogance. For his best friend and chief advisor Rajah Birbal, these rare lapses offered a chance to remind Akbar that, despite his great empire and all of his wealth, he was just a person like any other. So when one morning, after one of their long walks, Akbar attempted to better his advisor with a childish trick, Birbal decided to teach his friend a valuable lesson about life.

It began when Akbar challenged Birbal, as they sat drinking fresh, cool water in the palace gardens.

'Tell me, Birbal,' said Akbar, 'do you know how many bangles your wife wears?'

Birbal shrugged. 'I cannot say that I've given it much thought,' he replied. 'Bangles are bangles, after all.'

'Ha!' Akbar exclaimed with pride verging on arrogance. 'So, you see her hands every day yet you do not notice how many bangles she wears. How can that be?'

Birbal, feeling annoyed, took a deep breath. 'Your Majesty,' he replied softly. 'Let us take a walk by the lake and I will explain.'

They finished their drinks and walked through the gardens and on to the path that surrounded the lake. The water shimmered in the sunshine and everywhere birds chorused in the trees and shrubs. At the far end, a small stone staircase led up to the emperor's private residence.

'You take these stairs every day, Your Majesty,' said Birbal. 'Tell me, how many steps are there?'

The emperor shook his head. 'I see what you are saying,' he said, 'but it is not the same thing. We do not notice *things* as much as we notice the people around us. Your wife is a person, not a staircase and you should know how many bangles she wears. Besides, I own everything, so I don't care if there are six steps on this staircase or twenty. Nor do I care if there are two roses on a certain bush, or many more. They are all mine, regardless.'

Birbal shrugged. 'Very well, Your Majesty. I must attend to my duties. May I be excused?'

Akbar grinned. 'What?' he asked. 'No response or new lesson? Perhaps I am becoming as clever as you, dear friend?'

'Perhaps,' said Birbal, before walking away.

The following evening, Akbar was strolling past the lake to his quarters, when he spotted a vagrant lying in his rose bushes. Disbelieving, he edged closer and saw that the man was a sadhu – a holy man – dressed in ragged clothing and a once-saffron turban now dulled with grime.

'You!' he barked. 'How dare you lounge so carelessly in my gardens! GUARDS!'

The sadhu raised his head but did not reply.

'You!' Akbar said again, wondering where his guards had gone. 'Get out of here this instant!'

Sleepily, the old man shrugged, stroking his ragged beard. 'Is this *your* garden, then?' he asked.

'Of course!' Akbar replied. 'This garden, the palaces that surround it, the lake, the trees, this entire kingdom belong to me!'

'And what of the mighty river to the east, or the jungles to the south?' the sadhu asked. 'Are they *yours* too?'

'YES!' cried Akbar. 'Do you know who I am?'

The sadhu shook his head. 'I know not,' he replied. 'And I care not . . .'

'But . . .'

'Ssh!' the old man ordered. 'Tell me this, oh splendid

and wealthy man – to whom did these things belong before you?'

Akbar raised an eyebrow, and in that instant, his anger subsided and his curiosity grew. Who was this strange holy man with his questions? Akbar wondered if the man was a friend of Birbal's. It would be just like his friend to test the emperor so. Regardless, Akbar was a thoughtful person, prone to philosophical debate and open to the thoughts and words of others. Perhaps he could reason with this man, and show Birbal that his was a truly inquisitive mind.

'Did Birbal send you?' he asked.

'I know not this Birbal,' the sadhu said. 'And I care not. Answer my question. Who owned these things before you?'

'Why,' said Akbar, 'my father, of course. You must have heard of the mighty Emperor Humayun?'

'No,' the sadhu replied. 'I have not. But tell me, then, who was here before your father?'

Akbar shook his head.

'That would be Emperor Babar – my grandfather . . .' he replied.

'And before him . . .?'

'I . . . I . . .' began Akbar.

'Think a moment,' said the sadhu. 'This garden, these roses, the lake, the palaces – these things are only yours during your lifetime – correct?'

'Well, yes, but . . .'

'And when you are gone, they will belong to your son, and his son after him, and so on . . .?'

'Yes, that's true, but . . .'

'Each person only owns these things for as long as they live on this earth, then?'

'Yes.'

The sadhu smiled, showing blackened teeth. 'We are but travellers in this world,' he told Akbar. 'We travel the road, and when we need shelter from the sun, we rest in the shade of a tree. But eventually we move on, friend. The tree, however, stays where it is, and shades the next traveller, and the next . . .'

Akbar found himself nodding. He had never considered such things, in such a way, before. He looked around at his beautiful, lush gardens, and at the magnificent building surrounding them. The old man was correct – Akbar was merely their latest owner, and he would not be the last.

'Oh, wise one,' he said. 'I hear your words and I agree with them.'

'Heed them carefully, then,' the sadhu replied. 'For each of us must die one day, and none will take these things with us. The world is not yours, or mine, friend. It belongs to us all . . .'

Akbar thought of his wealth, and the splendour in which he had spent his life, and he felt ashamed. His riches no more belonged to him than the water in a well, or the birds in the trees. To learn such a lesson, at the hands of this old man . . .

The sadhu stood wearily. 'But,' he said, 'if you insist I go, then I shall leave at once . . .'

'No, no!' said Akbar. 'Stay as long as you wish, and let us talk some more about the world.'

The sadhu smiled, and began to remove his turban. Then, spitting tree bark from his mouth, pulling away his fake beard and wiping his face clean, he turned to Akbar.

'Perhaps it would be better to continue indoors, Your Majesty.'

'Birbal – it's you!' Akbar exclaimed, and once again, he gave thanks that he had been blessed with such a wise and true ally.

'Now, Your Majesty,' said Birbal, 'about my wife's bangles . . .'

Akbar grinned sheepishly, shrugged and led his friend away.

A Tale of Two Challenges

As stories of Birbal's wit and intelligence spread throughout Emperor Akbar's kingdom, many challengers came forward. One, an arrogant and wealthy merchant named Raj Lal, believed Birbal to be a trickster who had duped Akbar. One day, whilst attending a court reception, Raj Lal took Birbal aside.

'You and I both know what you are,' he whispered to Birbal.

'Oh?' said Birbal. 'And what am I?'

'A charlatan,' Raj Lal replied. 'Whether it is magic or

some other trickery, you have fooled Akbar. No one can be as clever as you . . .'

Birbal, always calm and assured, merely smiled. 'Perhaps you might test me yourself?' he suggested.

Raj Lal thought for a moment. 'Yes!' he said. 'But I will set you a challenge away from the palace. You are too comfortable here. Maybe a new setting will show up your tricks.'

'It does not matter where you set the challenge,' said Birbal. 'I am always happy to oblige.'

Raj Lal sneered. 'Birbal,' he said. 'When you fail, your reputation will be ruined. I give you my word!'

Birbal said nothing.

Two days later, an invitation to lunch arrived from Raj Lal. Birbal dressed in his finest robes and made the short journey to the merchant's house. Akbar, unaware of Raj Lal's challenge, searched for his friend that afternoon.

'Have you seen Birbal?' he asked his personal guard.

'He left this morning, Your Majesty,' the guard replied. 'He did not say where he was going.'

A short while later, Birbal's fiercest court rival, Abdul Qadir, sought out the emperor.

'A holy man has arrived,' Abdul Qadir told Akbar. 'He wishes to test the intelligence of your court.'

Akbar had grown bored without Birbal, and loved a challenge. He was also proud of his courtiers, all of whom he had hand-picked. His nine councillors were amongst the cleverest and most capable in the entire kingdom.

'Bring him to me!' he bellowed. 'Let me meet this holy man!'

The bony holy man wore nothing but a cloth round his waist. He carried a mahogany staff and a pot that had been covered in cheesecloth. He placed the pot before Akbar and bowed.

'Your Majesty,' he said. 'I am humbled in your presence.'

Akbar waved his hand, as though he was swatting a fly. 'No need for pleasantries,' he said. 'You think you can outwit my court, do you?'

The holy man nodded. 'I mean no disrespect,' he said. 'I am just a modest man. My challenge is a test of intelligence, nothing more. I have heard great things of your councillors. I am convinced, however, that my test will defeat them.'

Akbar grew intrigued. 'What makes you think they will fail?' he asked.

'Because my challenge is unbeatable,' the holy man replied. 'I have travelled across Arabia and Persia, and into your lands, visiting every learned prince and king, and none have prevailed.'

Akbar smiled. 'Well, today you will meet your match,' he said. 'What is your challenge?'

The holy man pointed to the clay pot. 'I challenge your court to tell me what the pot contains,' he said.

Akbar's court fell silent.

'Fair enough,' said Akbar. 'If you win, I will give you one thousand gold coins. But if you lose, you will tell everyone you meet that Akbar's court is the wisest of all.'

'Agreed,' said the holy man.

One by one, Akbar's councillors stepped forward. His astrologer consulted various charts and declared the pot to contain nothing but water.

'Wrong,' said the holy man.

His chief finance minister suggested gold.

'Wrong,' said the holy man.

Akbar's prime minister came forward. 'This is impossible,' he said. 'We cannot guess what is in the pot. This challenge is unwinnable. Have this wretch thrown in jail, Your Majesty!'

Akbar shook his head. He had accepted the challenge in good faith. His reputation would not survive if he grew angry and jailed the holy man.

'Where is Birbal?' he whispered to Abdul Qadir.

'Who cares?' replied Abdul Qadir. 'We do not need him. I will win this challenge for you!'

But Abdul Qadir could not guess what the pot contained, despite many attempts. One by one, Akbar's entire court failed, and soon only Akbar himself remained . . .

Birbal, meanwhile, sauntered slowly back to court, having indulged in a sumptuous lunch. Raj Lal had provided roasted pheasant and curried goat, mountains of scented rice and spiced vegetables, followed by exotic and expensive fruits and nuts, and sticky sweetmeats. Raj Lal had been a very generous host. It was a shame that his arrogance had left him so embarrassed, however.

Raj Lal had set his challenge after lunch. Gesturing to Birbal, he cleared his throat so each of his numerous guests would hear.

'Today I, Raj Lal, will set the famous Birbal a challenge,' he announced. 'And he will not succeed. After this, I will forever be known as the man who defeated Birbal's legendary wit . . .'

The audience clapped and cheered wildly, all except for one man, who simply looked embarrassed. Birbal stood and asked Raj Lal to hurry up.

'I must get back,' he said. 'Set your challenge.'

Raj Lal smirked. 'Somewhere amongst this crowd is my only other guest,' he said. 'Your challenge is to pick him out.'

Birbal pretended to look confused. 'But I thought they were all guests,' he said.

'Haha!' said Raj Lal, beaming at his own genius. 'I have you beaten already, dear Birbal!'

Once again, everyone in the room guffawed and hooted in delight. All bar the same man as before.

'I don't understand,' said Birbal.

'The rest are my servants!' Raj Lal boasted. 'They all

work for me. Now tell me, supposed wise man, which is the only other guest?'

Birbal picked up a mango slice and swallowed it. The fruit was syrupy and utterly delicious.

'Well . . .?' asked Raj Lal, when Birbal failed to respond.

'I really did expect a more difficult challenge,' said Birbal, wiping mango juice from his chin.

He pointed to the only guest who hadn't clapped and cheered. Raj Lal's smile disappeared.

'B-b-but . . .!' he stammered, as the entire room fell silent.

'He is the only one who didn't cheer,' Birbal explained. 'So right away I knew that he was the guest. Your servants are paid to obey every command. He is not.'

Birbal grabbed a handful of pistachio nuts as the humiliated Raj Lal's face went red.

'Would you mind if I took these?' he said. 'I do *like* nuts . . .'

Akbar was almost ready to accept defeat when Birbal walked into court and belched.

'Do excuse me, dear Majesty,' he said. 'I think I ate too much for lunch.'

'Birbal!' said Akbar. 'This holy man has set a challenge that cannot be defeated. What can you do?'

Birbal shrugged. Next to Akbar, Abdul Qadir simmered with rage and prayed that Birbal would fail.

'Explain,' Birbal said to the holy man.

The holy man pointed at the clay pot.

'I challenge you to tell me what is inside the pot,' he said, before grinning.

Birbal took a pistachio from his pocket and began to peel away the shell. 'Hmmm . . .' he said. 'I must tell you what the pot contains?'

'Yes,' said the holy man.

'Just that, and nothing else?'

'Yes . . .'

'Very well, then,' said Birbal.

He approached the pot and tore off the cheesecloth covering it.

'Nothing,' he declared. 'Your pot contains nothing.'

'But you cheated!' the holy man yelled, as a wave of gasps encircled Akbar's court. Abdul Qadir was the only one smiling. Birbal would pay for this.

'Well?' asked Akbar. 'Why did you cheat?'

Birbal shrugged. 'I did not cheat,' he replied.

'Of course you cheated!' yelled Abdul Qadir. 'You are lying to the mighty Akbar!'

Birbal sighed. 'I did not lie,' he replied. 'I was asked to reveal what the pot contains. No one said that I couldn't look *inside* . . .'

Akbar's puzzlement turned to delight. Once again, Birbal had outwitted them all.

'But, but . . .' both Abdul Qadir and the holy man spluttered in unison.

'Enough!' Akbar declared. 'Take your pot and leave, holy man! And do not forget to tell the world that Akbar's court succeeded where all others failed!'

The holy man accepted defeat and left, as Abdul Qadir disappeared in a rage. Akbar turned to Birbal and grinned.

'You continue to surprise and delight me, dear friend,' he said.

'Thank you,' replied Birbal, taking more pistachios from his pocket. 'Would you care for a nut . . .?'

Birbal Goes Missing

One summer evening, feeling out of sorts, Emperor Akbar quarrelled with his best friend and advisor, Birbal. Their simple, petty argument ended with Birbal storming from the palace. He vowed never to return. In the heat of the moment, Akbar reacted childishly too. 'I don't care!' he yelled.

A hushed silence descended over Akbar's court, and in the shadow of a stone pillar, Abdul Qadir, always envious of Birbal's position, smirked at his opponent's misfortune. 'Good riddance!' he whispered.

Within two days, however, Emperor Akbar regretted

his words. He missed his best friend greatly, and wished he would return. The pleasures of court – vast banquets and wonderfully melodious music, dancers, jesters and performing animals – did nothing to assuage his sorrow. He had to find a way to regain Birbal's friendship.

Akbar had nine advisors at court, of which Birbal was the most trusted. Now he turned to his others for help. Each man offered little, until it was Abdul Qadir's turn to give advice. The last thing Abdul desired was Birbal's return.

'I took the liberty of searching for Birbal, Your Majesty,' Abdul said. 'I know that you and he are close, but I fear he has gone for good . . .'

'No!' Akbar cried. 'It was just a squabble. Why would he leave?'

Abdul sensed his chance and took it. 'Perhaps he isn't the man you believe him to be?' Abdul suggested. 'Perhaps he does not value his position as greatly as he might?'

'You dare to question my judgement?' Akbar demanded to know. 'I brought him to court . . .'

Abdul, red-faced and suddenly anxious, backtracked with speed. 'No, no, Majesty!' he insisted. 'Not *your* judgement. I question the loyalty of Birbal . . .'

Akbar dismissed Abdul with a wave of his hand. 'I will find him!' he declared. 'I will make this right.'

With five soldiers by his side, Akbar rode his horse to

Birbal's house, where he found the door locked. One of his men peered through a window.

'It is empty, Your Majesty,' the soldier said. 'Not even a mouse stirs within.'

Akbar felt great sorrow rising inside his chest. 'My dear Birbal,' he whispered. 'What have I done?'

When a week had gone by, and Birbal failed to appear, Akbar had a brainwave. 'Abdul Qadir!' he bellowed.

The snake-like courtier emerged from the shadows at once, his head bowed. 'Yes, Your Majesty?'

'Tell me, do you understand the maxim that it *takes* a thief to *catch* a thief?'

Abdul's legs began to shake. Was the emperor accusing him of stealing . . .?

'But, Your Majesty, I . . .'

'Silence!' Akbar replied. 'I'm not accusing you of anything. I have an idea.'

'An *idea* . . .?' asked Abdul with barely concealed distaste.

He resembled a man chewing on an angry hornet. As far as Abdul was concerned, too many fancy *ideas* were discussed around court, all thanks to the outsider, Birbal.

'I declare the following,' said Akbar. 'A thousand gold coins to any man who comes to the palace, satisfying certain conditions . . .'

'Conditions . . .?'

'Yes,' Akbar told him. 'The man must walk in the sun, without an umbrella, yet still be in the shade.'

'But that is impossible,' said Abdul.

'For a man of your limited intellect, perhaps,' Akbar replied. 'Birbal might think otherwise, however. I certainly hope so.'

Abdul held his anger at bay, fearful of a dark prison cell. 'Do you wish to see every wretch who will try to claim a reward personally?'

Akbar smiled. 'No, no,' he said. 'After all, why do I pay my advisors? Disturb me only if Birbal comes back. And he *will* . . .'

Abdul smiled, as a plan formed in his mind. 'Certainly, Your Majesty,' he replied. 'I shall take care of everything!'

'Good fellow,' said Akbar.

Many, many people journeyed to court, each to claim the reward. Women came with sari fabric wrapped round their faces, and men wearing half-formed turbans. Yet none of them met Akbar's conditions. Abdul set up a side room, well away from the emperor's eyes, and took personal charge of assessing every claim. He was inundated and grew increasingly angry as each day passed. Was there no end to greedy people, hungry for gold coins?

'Enough!' he cried on the seventh day. 'I shall go and tell the emperor that his idea has not worked.'

'But, sir,' said one of Akbar's guards. 'There is a man in the courtyard.'

Abdul sighed. 'Is he the last?'

'For today,' the guard replied.

'Then send him in . . .' Abdul wearily replied.

The man was wretched beyond imagination. Wearing only a cloth dhoti and caked in mud and Lord knows what else, he walked in holding aloft a traditional woven bed – a charpoy.

'Failed,' said Abdul without looking up.

The man set down his charpoy and challenged Abdul's dismissal.

'But, sir,' he said. 'I walked here in the sun, yet the strings of this charpoy gave me shade too. I have satisfied all of the emperor's conditions. I deserve my reward.'

Abdul looked up then, and studied the wretch. Who-ever the man was, he did not seem to be Birbal.

'Nonsense!' Abdul replied. 'Now be gone before I have you thrown in jail!'

The man did not protest. Lifting his charpoy once again, he trudged out, stopping only to wink at the guard.

When Akbar learnt of his plan's failure, he grew des-pondent. 'Not a single person?' he asked Abdul Qadir.

'I'm sorry, Majesty,' Abdul replied. 'No one passed your test, and not one of them was Birbal. I fear he is gone for good . . .'

'But we are friends,' Akbar said.

'It pains me deeply,' Abdul lied, 'to think that my emperor has been disrespected so. He could not have been a true friend . . .'

Akbar did not hear Abdul, however; such was his sorrow. 'Was there no one . . .?' he asked again.

A guard coughed. 'Er . . . Your Majesty?'

'Who said that?' Abdul demanded. 'Silence!'

'No, no,' Akbar said. 'Let him speak.'

The young guard stepped forward. 'I saw one man, Your Majesty,' he revealed. 'He was the last to appear. I think it was Birbal but I cannot be sure.'

'Why mention him?' asked Abdul. 'If you are not sure?'

The guard waited nervously for the emperor to grant him permission.

'Go on . . .' said Akbar.

'Well, the man was caked in filth,' he said. 'But on his way out, he winked at me . . .'

Akbar's grin was wide and dazzling. 'He *winked* at you?'

'Yes, Your Majesty . . .'

'Birbal!' Akbar exclaimed.

'B . . . but . . . I saw this man!' said Abdul. 'He looked nothing like Birbal!'

Akbar ignored Abdul. 'Go and fetch him at once – wherever he is!' he ordered his guards.

*

When they returned hours later, the wretched man had not changed. His face and body were plastered in dried mud, and his dhoti was just as filthy. Above his head, he still carried the charpoy. Akbar, amused at his friend's charade, demanded to know why he should be given the reward.

'I walked here in the sun,' the man replied. 'But still this charpoy gave me shade . . .'

Abdul Qadir stood open-mouthed, his face red.

'My dear Birbal!' Akbar replied. 'Wash off that mud and you may collect your reward. It is good to have you back, dear friend . . .'

Birbal put down his charpoy and wiped the mud from his eyes. Noting how Abdul Qadir squirmed, he smiled.

'It is good to be back, Your Majesty,' he said.

Birbal's Khichri

One exceptionally cold winter morning, Emperor Akbar and his chief advisor, Birbal, took a stroll through the palace gardens. Laid out in ornate patterns, and planted with expert skill, the gardens pleased Akbar even in the depths of such a bitter season. Beyond the gardens, past a wall that in summer was thick with climbing vines and roses, lay a beautiful lake surrounded on three sides by a forest of evergreen trees. Around the bark path several oil lamps stood, ready to light the way in darkness.

As they walked, Birbal wondered about the greed of men.

'Your Majesty,' he said, 'do you think there is anything a man would not do for money?'

Akbar, used to such questions from his loyal friend, took a moment before replying. He crouched and put his hand into the water. It was icy and bit to the bone. Hastily withdrawing his fingers, he smiled.

'I should imagine there are some things,' he said. 'Who would spend all night in this freezing lake, for example?'

Birbal liked a challenge, and thought he had heard one.

'I shall find such a man,' he told Akbar.

'Pah!' scoffed the emperor. 'If you find anyone so willing, I shall reward that person with a thousand gold coins!'

Birbal set about his task immediately. Wrapped in a thick blanket to ward off the chill, he left the palace to begin his search. From one village to the next, Birbal sought someone willing to take on the emperor's challenge, but to no avail. Then, after two fruitless days, and all but resigned to failure, he chanced upon a desperately poor wretch. Dressed in nothing but a ragged and rough sheet, barefoot and half starved, the poor man jumped at such a chance.

'My wife and children have no food,' he told Birbal. 'They will surely starve if I do not find some money. I will do it!'

'But what of the danger?'

The poor man shook his head, his hair knotty with

dirt. 'I must do what I can,' he replied. 'For the sake of my family.'

Birbal agreed and led him back to Akbar's palace. When the poor man saw the lake, a feeling of terror overtook him.

'If you wish to walk away,' Birbal told him, 'you may do so.'

The poor man, mindful of his family's desperation, declined.

'Is this the fellow?' Akbar exclaimed, as he reached the lake.

'Your Majesty!' the pauper gasped, falling to his knees at once.

'Do you agree to enter this trial voluntarily?' Akbar asked the man.

'Yes, Your Majesty, I do.'

'Then let good fortune smile on you.'

They watched the man enter the lake, and after posting a guard to keep watch on him, Akbar and Birbal left.

The next morning, the guard brought the wet and shivering wretch to Akbar.

'Did you spend the entire night as you said?' Akbar asked, astonished that the man had not succumbed.

'Yes, Your Majesty.'

The guard confirmed his story, as Abdul Qadir stepped forward. This man, jealous of Birbal's growing influence, saw an opportunity to gain favour with Akbar at Birbal's expense.

'What sorcery is this?' Abdul asked. 'How could anyone survive a night in the lake, Your Majesty? I fear subterfuge . . .'

Akbar held the man's gaze once more.

'Well?' he demanded. 'Did you use anything to help you win your challenge?'

The poor man shook his head.

'I did as you asked,' he repeated. 'I concentrated on the closest oil lamp to keep my mind from the cold.'

'You see?' said Abdul. 'Lies!'

'Aha!' cried Akbar. 'Then it is true! You kept warm by the oil lamp and have failed your challenge!'

'But Your Majesty . . .'

'Enough!' Akbar told him, much to the delight of the wily Abdul. 'There shall be no reward. Away with you!'

Distraught and bewildered, the poor man trudged wearily from court, and sought out Birbal.

'I did as you asked,' the man told Birbal. 'I have been cheated.'

Birbal told him to return to his family. 'You shall have your reward very soon,' he promised. 'I give you my word.'

Two days passed and Birbal was not seen at court. On the third day, a perplexed Akbar sent a messenger to find his absent friend. The messenger returned to tell Akbar that

Birbal was at home, waiting for his khichri to cook. Once it was done, Birbal would return to court. Confused, but by now used to Birbal's eccentricities, Akbar waited. And waited and waited . . .

After many hours, Akbar decided to visit Birbal himself. The wily and envious Abdul Qadir accompanied him, alongside several attendants. Akbar found his friend sitting cross-legged, watching over a small fire of twigs. Suspended high above was a bowl filled with rice. Akbar was amused.

'Your rice is too far away from the fire, friend,' he said. 'It will never cook like that!'

He burst into laughter, and Abdul followed suit. When Birbal failed to react, Akbar grew confused.

'Birbal,' he said, 'how can it possibly cook with the flame so distant?'

Birbal shrugged.

'As a man in a lake might be warmed by the light of a lamp?' he asked.

'You cannot speak to His Majesty in that manner!' Abdul cried. 'Who do you think you are?'

'I'm merely a man who wishes to tell the truth,' Birbal said. 'It does not matter to whom I tell it. Truth is truth.'

Amid gasps from his attendants, Akbar realized at once his mistake.

'My dear Birbal,' he said. 'Yet again, you have taught me

a lesson. Where is the poor man I have wronged so dreadfully? I shall give him his reward at once!'

Birbal stood and doused the flames with a pitcher of water. 'Come, Your Majesty,' he replied. 'I shall lead you.'

Akbar, waving away Abdul's energetic protests, took Birbal by the arm. 'My dear friend,' he said, 'you have led me since the day we met. I pray that you never stop leading me.'

Birbal eyed Abdul and grinned. 'I will not stop, dear friend,' he replied. 'Unless I am stopped by someone else, of course . . .'

The Story of Laila and Ajeet

Young Prince Ajeet loved to hunt. Each day he would saddle his horse, grab his bow and arrows and ride through the vast forest on the edge of his father's kingdom. He was tall and handsome, and very brave, but his mother, the rani, still worried about him. For beyond the forest lay great danger.

'You must never go east,' she warned him, each and every day.

'But, Mother,' the Prince would reply. 'The forest is so big that I could ride for days and never find the edge.'

Yet his mother couldn't stop worrying. To the east lived

the most beautiful girl in all creation, Princess Laila. Her father was a wicked man, who ruled his kingdom with fear. Many young men wanted to marry Princess Laila, but none had succeeded. Whenever they approached her father, the wicked king would set them impossible tasks. And when they failed, he would execute them. The rani worried that Ajeet, if he ever saw Princess Laila, would fall madly in love with her.

'He will not go east,' Ajeet's father, the rajah, reassured her. 'He would never disobey you.'

But still the rani fretted. She knew that once dazzled by Princess Laila's beauty no man could forget her.

Prince Ajeet obeyed his mother for a long time, but one day his curiosity overcame him.

'I wonder what mystery lies to the east?' he said, as he trekked down an overgrown path in search of deer.

'You must not go there!' his steward warned. 'Remember your mother's warnings, sire!'

'Nonsense!' Ajeet replied. 'I have killed tigers and bears. What could possibly be more dangerous?'

Later, when his steward was busy, Ajeet gathered up his reins and sped away. He rode all day, and into the night, before finding shelter under a giant peepal tree. Tired and hungry, he ate some fruit, and then lay down to sleep.

In the morning squawking parrots awakened him. Eager to see them, he pushed his way through the dense undergrowth, emerging in a clearing. The birds were fantastically rich and vibrant, their feathers coloured scarlet or emerald, or the brightest of blues. The prince took his bow and an arrow, and aimed for the nearest, missing wildly. The birds flew off in an instant, all except for the largest, which stood on a branch and glared at him.

'How dare you shoot at me!' it said. 'I am the Parrot King, and I belong to the Princess Laila. When she hears of this, you will be sorry!'

The prince was shocked. 'But how can you speak?' he asked.

'I have always spoken,' the Parrot King replied.

'And this Princess Laila, who is she?'

The Parrot King laughed. 'I could tell you,' he said, 'but then you would die . . .'

'But why would I die?' asked Ajeet.

The Parrot King sighed. 'Very well,' he said, 'I will explain, but remember that I warned you.'

'Go on . . .'

'Princess Laila is the most beautiful girl in the world,' the Parrot King said. 'She is more radiant than the sun, more luminous than the moon. She is kind and generous, and her love knows no bounds.'

Ajeet wondered if such a girl could really exist.

'She does not sound dangerous to me,' he replied.

'Not her,' said the Parrot King, 'it is her father, the

wicked rajah, who is dangerous. Many young men have wanted to marry her. For each, the rajah has set an impossible task, and no man has ever succeeded. Each one has died.'

'But I can do anything!' Prince Ajeet boasted. 'I am young and strong, and I fear nothing.'

'My dear fellow,' the Parrot King replied, 'go home to your parents and forget Princess Laila. No good can come of it.'

When the Parrot King fell silent, the prince hung his head in sorrow and rode home. When he arrived, he took to his room, refusing to eat or speak for five days. His poor mother sat by his side, praying that her son would soon recover. On the sixth day, the prince finally spoke, and told his parents what the Parrot King had said.

'I *must* find this princess,' he insisted. 'I cannot sleep or eat because I dream of her.'

'No, my son!' the rani cried. 'I cannot lose you to such madness. You've never even seen this girl.'

'That's why I must go,' the prince replied. 'I must meet her. And I shall win her hand and marry her too.'

'You cannot!' said the rajah. 'I forbid you from leaving!'

The prince shook his head. 'I love and honour you both,' he said. 'But I have made my decision.'

The rajah sighed and nodded. Then he gave Ajeet his

strongest and swiftest horse to take with him. When he was ready to leave, his parents walked with him to the palace gates.

'Take these rupees with you,' the rajah said. 'You may need money on your journey.'

'Thank you, Father.'

'Dear son,' said the rani. 'Is there nothing I can say to stop you?'

'I'm sorry, Mother,' the prince replied. 'I must go.'

The rani sobbed, taking a handkerchief and wrapping inside it some sweetmeats.

'Take these, my son,' she said to him. 'Eat them if you grow hungry and never forget my love for you.'

Saddened but determined, the young prince set off towards the east. He rode and rode, crossing the great forest, past the parrots, into a new land. There he waded through a river and climbed a hill, before descending into a jungle. He found shade under some mighty coral trees next to which sat a stone tank. It was full of fresh, clean water, so he bathed himself and watered his horse, before resting.

Taking the handkerchief from his tunic, he took out a sweetmeat and savoured its rosewater scent. He was about to eat it when he noticed an ant stuck to the sugary surface. Dropping it, he picked a new piece, but this one was crawling with more ants.

'No!' he cried.

Every piece of sweetmeat was infested with ants. He watched as they crawled around, and calmed down.

'These ants are just doing what comes naturally,' he said aloud. 'Let them eat, for they must be hungry too.'

He felt something crawl along his legs and up his torso. It was a large black ant. Holding out his hand, he let the ant crawl on to his palm.

'Excuse me,' said the ant. 'I heard what you said and I wanted to thank you.'

'But how can you speak?' Ajeet asked.

'I am the Ant Queen,' the little insect replied. 'I have always spoken. You have been very kind. Most people would have killed my workers. But you showed them great kindness.'

'It is no matter,' the prince said.

'I am in your debt,' the Ant Queen replied, 'if you ever need my help, just ask for me. I can appear anywhere.'

Ajeet thanked the Ant Queen, and was told of a nearby mango tree. He found it and ate until he was full. In the morning, the Ant Queen reappeared and bade the prince farewell.

Ajeet rode on for two days until he came to a deep valley. There he discovered a magnificent tiger with a thick thorn in its foot. Its roars echoed through the trees, scaring anything that heard them. Ajeet hid his horse and then drew his sword. As he approached, the tiger shook its huge head.

'Please,' it said, 'put your weapon down. I won't harm you.'

'But you are a tiger,' said the prince. 'You will eat me.'

'I am in terrible pain,' the tiger replied. 'I cannot walk. If the hunters find me, I will surely be killed. Please help me, I beg you!'

The prince sheathed his sword and edged closer still. The thorn had gone deep into the tiger's paw.

'Do you promise not to eat me?' the prince asked.

'Of course!' the tiger promised. 'On the lives of my cubs, I swear!'

The prince took a little knife from his pocket and started a small fire. Once ready, he heated the blade and told the tiger to hold very still.

'This will hurt,' he explained, 'but the thorn will be gone.'

'I am ready,' the tiger replied. 'Please, just hurry.'

Carefully, the prince cut out the thorn. The tiger's roar was so loud that far away, his wife heard and came rushing to help.

'Thank you, kind sir,' the tiger said. 'But please hide before my wife arrives.'

'Why?' asked the prince.

'If she sees you, she will attack you,' the tiger replied. 'Let me explain your kindness to her.'

The prince climbed high into the nearest tree, reaching safety just as the tiger's wife appeared.

'What human did this to you?' his wife bellowed. 'Show me, and I will tear out its heart!'

'No, no!' said the tiger. 'I stepped on a giant thorn and was in agony until a young man saved me.'

The tiger's wife stopped pacing and sat down. 'A human *saved* you?' she asked in utter astonishment.

'Yes, dear,' her husband replied. 'He is hiding in the tree above you, scared that you might kill him.'

The tiger's wife looked up and saw Ajeet. 'Do not fear me, young man,' she said. 'Come down, so I can thank you.'

Slowly and uncertainly, the prince descended. Wary of being attacked, he held his ground. But when the tiger's wife saw him, she nuzzled her head against his legs.

'How can I ever thank you?' she asked. 'If my husband had died, I would have been left all alone with my cubs.'

Ajeet shook his head.

'I could not let your husband suffer,' he said. 'I love to hunt, but not like this. It would have been dishonourable.'

'Then we can be friends . . .' the tiger's wife replied.

Ajeet stayed with the tigers for three days, making ointments for the husband's paw, and playing with the cubs. When it came time to move on, the tigers thanked him again.

'If ever you are in trouble, think of me, and I will come to you,' said the tiger. 'I am forever in your debt.'

The prince rode on, over the hills, and into another jungle. As he searched for a place to rest, he spied a gang of fakirs, or holy men, arguing. In front of them lay a bed, a bag, a stick and rope, and a stone bowl. Curious, Ajeet hid and watched the men quarrel.

'They are mine, I tell you!' said one of the men.

'No, no!' said the next. 'These magical possessions have always been mine!'

The third pulled a knife and began to threaten the others. 'Get away, you vile hounds!' he yelled.

The fourth tackled the third, and both men, already filthy, fell into a muddy puddle. Still they tussled and argued, until finally they grew tired.

Intrigued, Ajeet stepped from the shadows. 'Do not argue,' he said to the fakirs. 'Holy men should not be so greedy.'

The four holy men stopped arguing and gathered together. Unknown to Ajeet, they were actually bandits. And they loved nothing more than new victims.

'*Look at his fine clothes,*' whispered the first.

'*And that mighty sword,*' said the second.

'*We'll take everything he has,*' said the third.

'*Yes, but his magnificent horse will be mine alone!*' added the fourth.

Then the first bowed. 'I am so terribly ashamed,' he lied. 'My apologies, young man.'

Ajeet smiled. 'Don't worry,' he replied. 'We can find a better way to end your argument.'

The first fakir grinned. 'You are very wise,' he said. 'But you look tired and hungry. Won't you stay with us and take dinner?'

Ajeet, charmed by the offer, accepted at once.

'Fetch the bowl!' the first fakir demanded.

'But we cannot . . .' began the second, only for the third to interrupt.

'*What will he do?*' the third fakir whispered. '*Tonight we will slay him. So what if he discovers the magic bowl?*'

When Ajeet asked what they'd said, the first fakir shrugged.

'Oh, nothing,' he lied. 'We were just discussing the bowl's magical powers . . .'

'Magic?' the prince replied. 'Really?'

'Oh yes,' said the first fakir. 'But you must not tell a soul!'

Ajeet nodded. 'Of course,' he replied. 'I would never break your trust.'

The first fakir took the bowl. He asked for plates of coconut rice and curried goat, spiced okra and pineapple chutney. For dessert, he demanded rice pudding and mangoes. And to Ajeet's astonishment, everything suddenly appeared.

'Amazing!' said the prince. 'You are very fortunate to have these gifts.'

'*More fortunate than the dead rajah who last owned them!*' whispered the fourth fakir to the third. Both men broke into guffaws before a withering look from the first fakir ended their fun.

They ate heartily, and Ajeet told them his story. In return, the fakirs invented tales of their own generosity and bravery. Soon Ajeet was shown to a hammock, strung between two branches of a peepal tree. It was outside the fakirs' camp, but Ajeet was very grateful. He was tired and longed for sleep.

'Don't worry,' said the first fakir. 'This hammock is very relaxing. If you need us, just call out.'

Ajeet found sleep impossible. He tossed and turned, and could not relax. Finally, he went to fetch some water. The moon was high but partially hidden behind a cloud, so he trod carefully, anxious not to wake his hosts. But when he reached the camp's edge, he gasped in horror and hid.

The four men sat in a circle, with their knives drawn. They had slain Ajeet's mighty horse and roasted it on their fire. Their mouths were greasy with its flesh and Ajeet overheard their plan to kill him too. Then they began to argue again.

'The magic bed is mine!' said the first fakir. 'I'm tired of walking for days on end. The bed will take me anywhere I want to go!'

'Have it!' said the second, who was larger than the rest. 'I only want the stone bowl. My belly rumbles with hunger.'

'The charmed bag is mine,' the third declared. 'I can ask it for riches, and live like a king!'

'What about me?' the fourth fakir asked. 'The stick and the rope might attack anyone I ask, but so what? I want the magic bag!'

They continued their quarrel, revealing their secrets to Ajeet, who quickly devised a cunning plan. He ran to the hammock for his bow and arrows. On his return, the fakirs were holding their knives, ready to fight each other.

'Wait!' the prince cried, stepping out from behind a bush.

'Stand back, young man!' said the first fakir. 'You are our guest. We don't want to hurt you.'

'*Not until we are ready to hurt you ourselves!*' whispered the second.

'SSSSHHHHH!' the rest replied, but this time Ajeet heard clearly.

Pretending he hadn't heard, however, the prince continued, 'But you don't have to fight,' he said. 'My father was a wise man and taught me many things. I can settle your argument.'

The first fakir looked intrigued. 'Pray, do tell,' he said, showing blackened teeth and rotting gums. 'We would be entirely grateful . . .'

'*Until you meet your end, that is,*' whispered the third fakir.

'Silence!' growled the first.

Ajeet smiled.

'I will set a simple task for each magical possession,' he said. 'And whoever wins the task, gets that item.'

When he saw the confusion on their faces, Ajeet realized how truly brainless they were. *Perfect*, he thought. 'Each item will have its own arrow,' he continued, as though explaining to children. 'The bed, the bag, the stone bowl, and the stick and rope together. I will fire one arrow at a time, into the trees. The four of you will run to retrieve it. Whoever returns with an arrow, will receive the item to which it belongs. Is that clear?'

The fakirs nodded eagerly.

'So,' said Ajeet. 'Bring the items here at once, and we'll begin.'

Once the magical objects were assembled, the prince drew his first arrow.

'This one is for the bed,' he said, firing it into the trees.

The fakirs set off at once. They were not gone long before the first returned with the arrow. 'Aha!' he cried. 'The bed is mine!'

Ajeet fired the second arrow, this time for the bag. Once again the men ran off, and this time the second fakir was victorious.

'No need for quarrels,' he said. 'The bag belongs to me!'

The third arrow, for the stone bowl, flew off at speed. This time, the fakirs were gone a while. The portly fakir returned first. 'Those hounds ran the wrong way!' he gleefully said. 'Here is your arrow. The stone bowl is mine!'

Once all the men were back, Ajeet smiled. 'Now for the final race.'

The prince drew his string until the bow was almost at breaking point. He aimed further and higher than before, and in a completely new direction. When he let go, the arrow sailed and sailed, and soared and soared, covering a great distance. The fakirs, tired after the first three races, set off less swiftly than before.

Ajeet chuckled, before gathering the magical items together on the bed and climbing aboard. 'Magic bed, take me to Princess Laila's kingdom at once!' he ordered.

The bed rose high above the trees and carried the prince away with astonishing speed. Down below, the bogus fakirs returned to find their treasures gone. They howled and wept, and cursed their own greed and stupidity.

When the bed landed, Ajeet gathered together the smaller treasures in his bag. Then, strapping the bed to his back, he searched for a resting place. Soon he came across a rice farmer.

'Where am I, kind sir?' he enquired.

'This is Princess Laila's kingdom,' said the farmer. 'Why are you here?'

'To win her hand,' Ajeet replied.

'You are a fool,' the farmer said. 'Leave this place at once, or you will regret it!'

The prince thanked the man but walked on. At the outskirts of a splendid city, he found a deserted house. It was draughty and dusty, but perfect for his needs. Ajeet put down his treasures and fell fast asleep.

He awoke to darkness. Searching the place, he found a lamp, which he lit. He took the magic bowl and asked it for chicken, rice and water. The food appeared instantly, and he ate and drank until he was full. Then, eager to find Princess Laila, Ajeet went out to explore the city. His route took him towards the royal palace, but he saw few people. The streets and lanes were empty, save for a few guards. Sensing that he might be in danger, Ajeet hid in the shadows, directly below the palace roof.

Suddenly, he heard someone walking on the tiles above. He peered up and gasped. He saw a girl so beautiful that his heart jumped. She was extraordinary; her hair was long and jet black, and shimmered in the moonlight, her sandalwood-tinted skin was smooth and glowing with health, and her eyes were like emerald stars shining in the heavens. She wore a scarlet silk robe, and across her head she'd placed a band of diamonds and pearls. Ajeet fought back the urge to call her name, but he knew who she was immediately – Princess Laila!

The following evening, Ajeet returned and watched

Princess Laila again. If anything, she seemed even lovelier and Ajeet had to turn away. Princess Laila began to sing a soft, sad song about a caged bird. Her voice was like an angel's and brought a tear to Ajeet's eye. She sang of being a prisoner, and of finding her true love, and the prince fell hopelessly in love. Waiting until she left, he raced back to the magic bed.

'Take me to Princess Laila's room,' he urged, grabbing the stone bowl.

Soon he was watching his princess sleep. He took the bowl, and whispered to it. 'Rose-water halva and tangerine curd,' he said. 'Ripe and juicy mangoes, and sweet rice flavoured with coconut cream and cinnamon.'

He said a prayer and left the feast as a gift. Late the next morning, the princess awoke to a mountain of delicious desserts. Stunned and delighted, she began to eat. When her handmaiden arrived, she asked about the food.

'I thought you had sent them for me,' Princess Laila replied.

'Not I, dear princess,' said the servant.

'Then perhaps my mother wanted to surprise me,' Laila said. 'Won't you stay and have some too?'

The next day, as the princess slept late, Ajeet reappeared in her bedchamber, holding the magic bag.

'Make me a shawl as breathtaking and perfect as my love,' he said.

And from the bag he produced a garment woven of rare golden spider silk, embroidered with flowers and jewels, and sprinkled with stardust. Ajeet placed it on her bed and left. When the princess awoke and spied the shawl, she squealed in delight.

'Where did that come from?' asked her mother, the rani.

'I don't know,' the princess replied. 'Perhaps a gift from the gods . . .'

'You are blessed, sweet child,' said the rani. 'Such a treasure, indeed!'

Yet although she loved the shawl, the princess had more than enough clothes. She summoned her handmaiden and gave it to her.

'Keep this for your wedding day,' she said. 'Your husband will gasp in awe!'

'But, princess, this belongs to you,' the servant protested.

'It is yours,' Princess Laila said, smiling warmly. 'I insist, dear friend!'

On the third night, Ajeet asked his magic bag for a beautiful ring. When it appeared, he took one of Laila's delicate hands and placed the ring slowly and carefully. But he was not cautious enough, and the princess awoke with a fright.

'Who are you?' she asked. 'And why are you in my room?'

'Please don't fear me, princess,' said Ajeet. 'I heard about you from the Parrot King. I am Prince Ajeet.'

'But . . .'

'I left my kingdom to find you,' he continued. 'I wish to win your heart and your hand in marriage.'

Princess Laila broke into a smile. 'You have been leaving me gifts,' she said.

'Yes, my princess,' said Ajeet. 'To delight you, as you delight me with your radiance.'

'Such lovely words,' the princess replied. 'But many men have said such things. Let me test you . . .'

'Anything, dear princess,' said Ajeet.

'Tell me,' she asked. 'Who is more beautiful, your mother or me?'

The prince was puzzled but answered anyway. 'You *are* truly beautiful,' Ajeet began. 'But my mother gave me life, and her hands cared for me. Even if she was an ogre, I would love her regardless.'

Laila's smile grew wider.

'My mother's beauty does not matter,' the prince said. 'And nor does yours. True beauty lies underneath the skin . . .'

The princess clapped her hands together and laughed.

'Come back tomorrow, so we can talk some more,' she said. 'But do not let my father catch you. He will kill you, if he finds out.'

And so, each day for a month, Ajeet and Laila met secretly and their love grew strong. But without her father's consent, Laila would never be able to marry Ajeet.

Then one morning, she made a confession to her mother. 'Mother,' she said. 'I have a great secret.'

The rani was puzzled. 'Secret?' she asked. 'What do you mean?'

'A handsome and noble prince has asked for my hand.'

'Then send him away!' cried the rani. 'Your father will kill him!'

'But we are in love,' Princess Laila replied, before revealing their secret meetings.

The rani, who longed for her daughter to find true love, broke down and wept. 'Then we must be brave,' she said. 'We must face your father and pray that Ajeet can succeed.'

The rajah exploded with fury when he heard the news. 'I do not care!' he said. 'This prince must pass my test or die . . .'

'Please, Father!' Laila begged. 'I cannot lose him.'

'That is your problem,' the rajah replied. 'Guards, find him at once!'

When Ajeet was arrested and dragged to court, he bowed his head and offered respectful greetings. The rajah grunted.

'Keep your greetings,' he snapped. 'You have dishonoured me and you will pay the price!'

'But, Father!'

'Silence!' the rajah bellowed. 'You are mine to give, child! Only I will decide your fate.'

Turning to Ajeet, the rajah sneered. 'I will devise a test

for you,' he said. 'Pass it, and you can have my daughter. Fail, however, and you will die.'

'If that is your command,' Ajeet replied. 'I won't fail.'

The rajah's attendants gasped at Ajeet's boast, and the rani grew faint. Princess Laila began to sob, and prayed that Ajeet would succeed.

'At sunrise, I will give you fifty kilos of mustard seed,' the rajah declared. 'And before the sun sets tomorrow, you must crush each one to draw out its oil.'

'I accept,' said Ajeet.

'No!' cried the princess. 'It is impossible. Father . . .!'

'Be quiet!' the rajah hissed.

Princess Laila sobbed and turned to her mother. 'No matter what happens, I won't stay in this wretched place!' she declared.

'Nor I!' said the rani.

At dawn, the rajah's men brought fifty kilos of mustard seed to the old house on a horse-drawn wagon. Dumping the seed, and clay pots for the oil, they withdrew with heads bowed. They, like all the people of the kingdom, hated to see their beloved princess so unhappy. Once the men were gone, Prince Ajeet smiled. Overnight, he'd formed a plan. Now he called out to the Ant Queen.

Within minutes, an army of ants crawled from every crack and crevice. There were millions of them, and the Ant Queen was at their head.

'My dear friend!' said the Ant Queen. 'You called so we came. What can we do?'

The prince explained his task and the Ant Queen nodded. 'No problem at all!' she declared. 'You take a nap. My workers will have this finished in plenty of time.'

And sure enough, before mid-afternoon, every last seed had been crushed and the oil collected. Ajeet thanked the Ant Queen and said goodbye. As quickly as they'd arrived, the queen's ant army vanished. When sunset came, the rajah arrived with his men. He was stunned to see the impossible task completed.

'Now I will marry my princess,' said Ajeet.

But the rajah grew angry and shook his head. He ordered his men to draw their swords.

'I cannot allow it!' he said to Ajeet. 'You have cheated – I'm sure of it!'

'But . . .'

'Another test or you die!' the rajah spat in rage.

'As you wish, Your Majesty,' Ajeet replied, as he was dragged back to the palace.

The princess wept when she saw her prince, and begged him to run.

'No!' Ajeet replied in defiance. 'He will not cheat us!'

The rajah smirked and then issued a new challenge. 'In my prison, I have two demons,' he told the prince. 'To marry my daughter, you must fight them and live.'

'I will,' said Ajeet.

Next morning, he was taken deep underground, to a dungeon so putrid that his stomach turned. Behind a locked door were the wicked rajah's demons.

'My demons await,' said the rajah. 'I shall return this evening. If you live, you shall have my daughter.'

'Do you swear on your honour?' Ajeet asked.

'Of course!' the rajah replied. 'Here, take these keys and enter, if you dare . . .'

The rajah chuckled, took his men and left, but Prince Ajeet did not panic. Once again, he had come up with a scheme. He sat down and called out to his friend, the tiger. Some hours later, the tiger appeared with his family. His cubs had grown strong and fierce, but became as playful as kittens on seeing Ajeet.

'Prince Ajeet,' said the tiger's wife. 'How can we help?'

Ajeet explained his problem and the tigers grinned.

'*Demons?*' roared the tiger's wife. 'They are no bother! You play with our children and we'll do the rest!'

When Ajeet unlocked the door, he heard snarls from the cell. His legs trembled slightly, but the tigers gave one ferocious roar and calmed his fears. They leapt into the cell and pounced on the monsters, tearing them to shreds in moments. Once done, they returned to their children.

'Lunch is served,' the mother said to her cubs. As her children ran in, she turned to Ajeet. 'Is there anything else – anything more *difficult*?'

'No, my magnificent friends,' Ajeet replied. 'Your debt to me is repaid.'

'Pah!' said the mother. 'That was nothing. We are still your servants.'

The tiger family stayed until just before dusk, before they slipped away into the gloom.

'I shall visit you soon,' the prince called after them, before covering himself in the demons' blood.

When evening came, and the rajah returned, he was apoplectic with rage.

'Impossible!' he bellowed. 'You cannot have survived!'

'But I am filthy with their blood,' the prince replied, showing the guards his terrible stains.

'I don't care!' the rajah cried. 'Guards, jail this man at once!'

Trembling in fear, the men locked Ajeet in the dungeon.

'I find you guilty of murdering my demons!' the rajah declared. 'Tomorrow morning, you die!'

When the princess heard of her father's treachery, she fell into depression. She begged to visit Ajeet but her father refused. The news spread rapidly across the kingdom, and there was great sorrow and rising anger. That night, Laila took to the roof, but did not sing. Instead, she wept in despair. Each of her falling tears turned to stone, until a pile was created as tall as the palace. Then, with a heavy heart she went to her bed.

During the night, though, she dreamt of a goddess, who explained how she could save Ajeet. When she woke up, she rushed to her mother.

'I must see Ajeet!' she cried. 'I have an idea!'

Then the rani called to her personal guard. 'Will you help us?' she asked him.

The guard nodded.

'I am your servant,' he said, 'as are the other guards. Ask us, and we shall do your bidding.'

Then he led Laila and her mother to the dungeon . . .

Just before noon, the prince was led to the palace gardens. There he was tied to a jackfruit tree. People had gathered from across the kingdom, but none were happy. When the rajah arrived, dragging his wife and daughter along, the crowd began to murmur in disapproval. The rajah, so pompous and wicked, did not notice their displeasure. Instead, he summoned his executioner.

'Today this prince will die,' the rajah bellowed, before inventing his crimes. 'He has been found guilty – of murder, and of practising witchcraft and cheating *me*. The sentence is death!'

Ajeet looked to Princess Laila and smiled. When the crowd saw this, many began to cry.

'Silence!' the rajah ordered.

Princess Laila had hidden her hair under a scarf. She

did not smile, instead lowering her gaze and saying prayers. Anger began to grow amongst the crowd.

'Axeman!' the rajah shouted.

The masked executioner strode forward with his powerful axe. He checked the ropes and then whispered to Ajeet.

'Fear not, noble prince,' he said.

With a mighty swing, he hacked at Ajeet's neck, where the rope was knotted most tightly. But the blade simply bounced off the twine and shot out of the executioner's hands, landing with a thud in a bed of yellow roses. Swiftly, each of the rajah's guards drew their swords, and the rani stepped forward.

'Take him!' she ordered.

But instead of Ajeet, the guards took hold of the rajah.

'What are you doing?' the rajah cried out in shock and fury. 'You filthy dogs – don't you dare touch me!'

The guards ignored his commands, dragging him to the very same dungeon into which Ajeet had been thrown. The rajah's subjects cheered and some threw ripe fruits. Laila ran to Ajeet, removing her scarf. The crowd saw her and gasped. Gone were her glorious locks, hacked short and sharp.

'I sacrificed my hair for my Ajeet,' she declared. 'From it, I fashioned the rope used to tie him. That is why the axe would not cut him.'

'But your wonderful hair!' came a cry.

'My hair will grow back,' the princess said. 'But I would never again have found true love.'

Soon afterwards, Laila and Ajeet were married, and their two kingdoms combined. Ajeet's parents were overjoyed to see him return, alive and well, and with his beautiful bride. For the rest of their days they lived in peace and happiness.

Of Water and Wells

Abdul Qadir, one of Akbar's advisors and the most vocal of Birbal's opponents at court, smiled. It wasn't a friendly smile. Instead, his expression was laced with arrogance, bravado and self-satisfaction. As he stood with a group of fellow courtiers, he could not help but grin.

'You are in a fine mood today, Abdul Qadir,' said one of his friends.

'I have been thinking,' Abdul replied. 'For too long this outsider, Birbal, has made us look foolish whilst ingratiating himself with the emperor . . .'

'He is too sharp, too clever,' said the man. 'We cannot get the better of him.'

Abdul shook his head. 'Not this time,' he replied. '*This* time I will outsmart Birbal! When I am done, Birbal will look the fool and Akbar will realize our true worth.'

Across the court, Akbar sat listening to a Sufi poet, with Birbal at his side. Before them, on a ruby silk sheet inlaid with golden thread, lay fancy goblets of pomegranate juice and silver platters of fruit and nuts. The poet's words were full of beauty, his rhythm mesmeric. He told of a gentle farmer's daughter crying. Of how her teardrops fell to the grass, glistening like morning dew until they dried into precious stones. Almost all at court were lulled by the magic of the poet's words. All but Abdul Qadir and his cohort.

A sudden disturbance by the great doors disturbed Akbar and made him angry.

'What is going on?' he demanded.

A young guard stood at the entrance, holding apart two quarrelling farmers.

'I'm sorry, Your Majesty, but these men would not stop.'

Akbar sighed. Although quick to anger, the emperor was keen to fulfil his duty to his subjects. Crowned at the age of thirteen, he had grown up with such things. A great ruler, his father had once said, rules for his people, not himself.

'Come forward,' he said. 'Let me hear them out.'

The two men lowered their heads in shame and came to stand before Akbar. The guard outlined their dispute.

'This is Moti Ram,' he said, pointing to a short, stout man with almost ebony skin and greying whiskers. 'He bought a well from Raj Singh.'

The second man was taller and fairer, and obviously wealthier. Whereas Moti Ram wore dirty rags, Raj Singh was dressed in much finer and cleaner fabrics.

'Then where is the problem?' Akbar asked the guard.

'Your Majesty!' Moti Ram begged. 'I paid him a fair price for the well, but now he demands that I pay him for the water too!'

'It is my water!' replied Raj Singh. 'I gave this wretch fair value for the well. I did not sell him the water too. I decide who draws my water . . .'

Akbar held up his right index finger. The men fell silent at once.

'I can see no issue here,' he said. 'Birbal . . .?'

His best friend and advisor took a grape from the platter and popped it into his mouth. As he chewed, he eyed both farmers.

'So, Moti Ram, it is your well?'

'Yes, sir,' Moti Ram replied. 'I paid a fair price – nearly all that I have.'

Birbal nodded. 'And you, Raj Singh?' he said. 'You insist you sold the well and not the water?'

'I do!' said Raj Singh. 'Where is the issue?'

Birbal took his time, eating another grape and taking a drink. 'Tell the guard where this well is,' he replied. 'Tomorrow, the emperor and I will visit you at midday. I shall give my verdict then.'

Unsatisfied, the men left, still arguing with one another.

'Sometimes I despair of this kingdom,' said Akbar. 'A well, indeed.'

'Despair not, Majesty,' Birbal replied. 'After all, what are your advisors for?'

Later, once the poet had finished his recital, Abdul Qadir took his chance. Approaching the emperor, he coughed into his hand.

'Yes, Abdul Qadir?'

'I have a great story for Your Majesty,' said Abdul. 'One that you will find most gloriously amusing . . .'

'Really?' Akbar replied. 'I've never considered you to be a great storyteller, Abdul.'

'Well,' said Abdul, feeling insulted, 'it was a dream I had – about Birbal. Perhaps you would like to hear it?'

'I would, yes,' said Akbar.

'Perhaps we should ask everyone to join us, then?'

Akbar agreed and the entire court stood silently, as Abdul Qadir cleared his throat. Birbal, showing little interest, ate a slice of ripe mango that dripped with sweet nectar.

'It was a moonless night, Your Majesty,' Abdul began.

'I found myself in the streets, when out of the shadows, I saw Birbal walking towards me, beckoning. I could not see his face, for his dark skin melted into the gloom all around me. Yet I could see the yellow of his teeth. As we approached each other, an owl hooted and Birbal jumped in fright. I, however, strolled on with purpose . . .'

Some of the courtiers began to giggle, and Abdul broke into a wide smile. Akbar sat motionless, a look of bemusement upon his face. Birbal, still feigning disinterest, cracked a nut between his teeth.

'It was so dark that we collided with one another and fell. Luckily for me, I fell into a pool of rice pudding, rich with cream and spices. But guess what Birbal fell into . . .?'

Akbar shrugged.

'Tell us, tell us!' shouted Abdul Qadir's friends.

'Very well, then,' said Abdul. 'Birbal fell into a gutter!!'

The court rocked with laughter. Some of the courtiers held on to each other. Others fell to the floor such was their amusement. Akbar smiled and turned to his friend, who was busy examining his fingernails.

'Birbal?' said the emperor. 'It seems that Abdul Qadir has made you the butt of an extremely funny story . . .'

Birbal took a swig of pomegranate juice before replying.

'It is indeed a very amusing tale,' he eventually said. 'But, by sheer coincidence, I had the exact same dream, Your Majesty . . .'

'Really?'

'Oh yes,' said Birbal. 'Only, unlike Abdul Qadir, I slept on until the very end . . .'

The laughter subsided, as everyone at court waited for Birbal to continue. Abdul felt a creeping sense of despair growing within. This was his time to shine. No one needed to hear from Birbal, the outsider.

'A likely story,' he blurted out. 'Your Majesty, I –'

'No, no, Abdul Qadir,' said Akbar. 'You've had your moment. Now we hear from Birbal. Do go on . . .'

'As Abdul climbed out of the rice pudding, and I from the putrid gutter,' said Birbal, 'we discovered that we had no clean water with which to wash . . .'

'Yes . . .?' Akbar asked, smiling slightly.

'Our only choice was to wash each other . . .' said Birbal, staring directly at Abdul Qadir.

'Each *other*?' said the Emperor.

'Yes,' replied Birbal. 'So we washed each other . . . with our *tongues*!'

The court exploded with laughter, and this time Akbar joined in. So intense was the shame and anger felt by Abdul Qadir, he turned and stormed from the room. As he went, the courtiers pointed and roared with amusement. Birbal, saying nothing more, picked up another grape and put it into his mouth . . .

The following day, as promised, Akbar, Birbal and two guards arrived at the disputed well. Both Moti Ram and

Raj Singh were calm, each of them hoping to be victorious over the other. Raj Singh had dressed in his very best clothes, and had his servant offer a gift of flowers and sweets to the emperor. Moti Ram, however, had nothing but the clothes that he had worn the previous day. His face was covered in a fine layer of flour dust, his hands were dry, and his head remained bowed.

'Raj Singh,' said Birbal, as he dismounted his horse. 'I wish to clarify the situation one last time before I give my advice.'

'Whatever your wish, sir,' Raj Singh replied. 'I know that my claim is honourable, and I have nothing to hide.'

Birbal nodded and walked over to the well. He patted the wall before peering down at the water. 'So this well belongs to Moti Ram?' he asked the wealthier man.

'It does,' Raj Singh replied.

'But the water remains yours, you say?'

Raj Singh nodded. 'Absolutely, sir,' he said. 'Moti Ram said nothing about buying the *water*, only the well . . .'

Moti Ram raised his head to complain, but Birbal told him to wait.

'So, in effect,' said Birbal, 'you, *Raj Singh*, are storing *your* water in Moti Ram's well?'

Raj Singh grew confused but nodded anyway.

'Well, yes, if you put it like that, I . . .'

'Moti Ram?' asked Birbal. 'Why, then, do you not charge Raj Singh *rent* for using your well?'

Moti Ram, realizing his victory, allowed himself a brief smile.

'Your Majesty?' said Birbal.

Akbar took a moment to appraise both men and then made his decision.

'Raj Singh,' he said. 'You shall pay Moti Ram rent for this well. Otherwise I order you to remove your water at once!'

'But, Your Majesty, this is preposterous!'

'I will not give my judgement again,' Akbar warned.

Raj Singh, outwitted and outnumbered, realized that he had no choice. He withdrew, but not before Akbar made him apologize to his neighbour. Once done, Akbar turned to Moti Ram.

'I have no need for flowers and sweets in this heat,' he told the poor farmer. 'But fresh, cold water would be like a blessing from heaven . . . do you happen to have any?'

The Blind Saint

One year, a blind saint arrived in Akbar's kingdom. The man was said to be able to see into the future and Akbar's subjects flocked to the saint's ashram, eager to know what fate held in store for them. As his reputation grew, the saint's powers made Akbar curious.

'There is no such thing,' Birbal replied, when Akbar asked him.

'But my subjects claim him to be accurate!' said Akbar. 'What harm could a visit do?'

Birbal smiled. 'In my experience,' he said, 'such men are merely charlatans and scoundrels. One day this saint will prove himself a sinner, and when that day comes, Your Majesty must not be connected to him in any way. Your reputation depends upon such things . . .'

Unhappy but wary of ignoring Birbal's advice, Akbar tried to forget his curiosity, but as with the monsoon rains, such moods came and went according to their own timetable. Nothing – not hunting nor feasting, nor the words and melodies of countless poets and musicians tamed Akbar's interest. He longed to find out if the saint was as his subjects claimed – a genuine teller of fortunes.

Over time, the saint grew fatter and richer, as people arrived from across the kingdom to hear his prophecies. Birbal, sure that his own prediction would turn out to be true, watched on, occasionally disguising himself as a beggar to visit this famed saint as an observer, but never presenting himself for a reading. It was on one such trip that Birbal's suspicions began to grow.

The ashram was full of devotees, each sitting cross-legged on either side of the saint – all of them under the shade of a huge tent. The man himself wore numerous garlands of marigold, jasmine and rose, and a robe of the finest ivory silk. His silver hair was rich with coconut oil, the skin of his hands soft and clean. Before him stretched a line of people, eager to speak with him. And all around were the spoils of his trade – fine fabrics and expensive dishes, delicious sweets and fruits, and mountains of nuts. A single wooden box sat at his feet, into which his patrons put money, and Birbal had no need to ask if it was full. He had observed so many people paying tribute that he wondered if the saint might not rival Akbar himself for wealth very soon. The saint reached out for a nut, his hand hovering for a moment before picking out a salted almond. Birbal watched the way the saint chose his treat with great care.

'He likes salted almonds,' Birbal whispered to the man standing next to him.

'They are his favourites,' said the man. 'He does not eat any other nuts . . .'

At the head of the line, Birbal spotted an old couple with a girl in tow. The child was no more than eight or nine years old, and completely dishevelled. The man spoke up.

'Oh, great saint,' he said. 'Please help us to understand what fate has decreed for our niece.'

The saint's head remained bowed, as though in deep contemplation. 'Continue, my son,' he whispered.

'My brother and his wife were murdered by bandits and we were left their daughter. She does nothing but sit and cry, and murmur wicked thoughts of revenge. Will she ever recover and marry a suitable man?'

The saint raised his head and turned it from side to side. He raised a hand to his eyes and rubbed them. 'I am but a blind old man,' the saint said. 'But I will do my best to alleviate your fears . . .'

'Thank you, great saint.'

'You will first make your offering, for without a gift to the heavens, the gods will not grant me their audience.'

'Anything you wish, oh blessed one!' the uncle cried. 'I have brought money and fruits and a dish made of gold . . .'

'Bring the child forward, that she might touch my feet, and me her face . . .'

Birbal watched the girl peer out from behind her long and knotted hair. Her eyes widened and her mouth fell open.

'YOU!!!!!!!!!!!!!!!' the girl screamed.

The saint flinched at the severity of her tone.

'It was you!!!!!' the girl continued. 'You killed my parents!'

The saint's devotees sprang to their feet, pushing the girl and her family away.

'Be gone!' screamed one of them. 'How dare you besmirch the sanctity of this ashram! If I were not so pious, I would chop off your heads!'

The couple turned and fled, with the girl behind them, as other patrons punched and kicked at them. Birbal withdrew a safe distance, and once the girl and her family were clear, he pulled them aside.

'Do as I say!' he ordered. 'Otherwise, I cannot save you!'

Behind them, two angry, vicious-looking devotees edged closer. Both looked like bandits pretending to be holy men – their skins scarred with needle tattoos, their ears heavy with gold rings.

'They must die!' said one.

'Long live the saint!' cried another.

Birbal removed the grimy turban he was wearing and shed his pauper's clothes to show the finery beneath.

'It is Birbal!' said the first devotee.

'Yes,' Birbal replied. 'And it is my duty to take these liars to the court of the emperor. Now, let us pass in safety or I shall call for the royal guards . . .'

The men stood aside and let Birbal and his party leave.

'They will pay for their crimes,' Birbal added, winking at the distraught uncle. 'But at the emperor's hand – not yours!'

The men nodded but their expressions grew yet more callous.

'Do not come back, lying scoundrels!' one warned. 'Next time Birbal will not be able to save you . . .'

At court, having left the couple and their niece in his chambers, Birbal sought out Akbar.

'What is it, old friend?' asked Akbar upon seeing Birbal's pained expression.

'The famous saint, Your Majesty,' replied Birbal. 'I fear I was correct in my warnings.'

'How so?' Akbar asked.

Birbal told him of all he had witnessed, and led him to

the poor girl he'd rescued. Upon seeing the emperor, the girl's uncle and aunt fell to their knees.

'Do not punish us!' they implored. 'We did not know the girl would make such wicked allegations!'

The girl showed no emotion, save for anger.

'I did not lie!' she insisted. 'It was that man and his gang who murdered my parents. If my mother had not hidden me in the water buffalo pen, I would have died too!'

Akbar took in the child's wild expression, her matted hair and her bare and filthy feet, and his heart cracked a little.

'But she is only young,' he said to her uncle and aunt. 'Why would she lie?'

The uncle looked up, trembling. 'I do not know, Your Majesty,' he stammered. 'She says so many things . . .'

'That man is a saint,' the aunt added. 'How could he be a murderer? I feel so ashamed . . .'

But the girl did not change her story. All day, and again the next morning, she insisted her words were true. Birbal and Akbar, after consulting privately, agreed that there was only one solution.

'Take her to the women's quarters,' Akbar ordered his guards. 'I want this poor child cleaned and fed at once!'

The girl struggled as the guards led her away, but could not match their strength.

'And you two may use these chambers for your own needs,' Akbar told the uncle and aunt. 'I shall send for the saint and in a few hours we will know the truth . . .'

The saint arrived with three of his devotees leading him. Birbal noted at once his change of clothes, from silken finery into dour and drab sackcloth. Gone were the golden earrings, the marigold, jasmine and rose garlands, and the cleanliness. Instead, his face, feet and hands were now covered in grime and mud. He walked with a stick, tapping it this way and that. Every so often, his followers corrected his path before he bumped into someone or something. Birbal even noticed a slight limp on the saint's left side.

Akbar sat on his throne, the girl and her family standing with guards to his right. Birbal stood at his left, chewing on a handful of pistachios and salted almonds.

'Saint,' said Akbar. 'I thank you for gracing my court with your presence.'

The blind saint fell to his knees but faced away from Akbar. Birbal smirked and ate some more nuts.

'It is I who have the honour,' said the saint, his tone meek. 'Oh, great Akbar, let me kiss your feet and offer thanks for your existence . . .'

'Yes, yes,' said Akbar. 'Let us get to the matter at hand.'

'Such a woeful mistake, Your Majesty,' the saint replied, as one of his followers turned him to face the emperor.

'I will not hold it against the poor child. She is clearly lost, her wits gone . . .'

'Nevertheless,' Akbar continued. 'A grave accusation has been made. Murder is strictly forbidden in my realm, and the punishment for such wickedness is death.'

Birbal stepped forward. 'As is the penalty for malicious and false accusations,' he added.

The girl's uncle gasped and her aunt let out a shriek. The girl did not react, however, her gaze firmly set on the saint.

'But there is no need for such things,' the saint said. 'I am happy to forgive this poor child her trespasses . . .'

Birbal shook his head. 'The law cannot be bargained with, nor must it be diluted,' he said. 'So I have devised a simple solution. We will hear the child's allegation, and then we will hear the saint's rebuttal. Once done, the court will decide who tells the truth. Does this strike you as fair, holy man?'

The saint nodded.

'Unless,' he said, 'there is a mistake, of course.'

'A mistake?'

'It is but her word against mine,' the blind man added. 'There is no proof.'

Before Birbal could reply, the girl shouted her reply. 'You murdered my parents!' she said. 'I don't need proof. I saw you kill them with my own eyes. As God is my witness, I –'

'ENOUGH!' roared Akbar.

The girl stopped at once and bowed her head. Birbal approached and took her hand. 'Come with me, child,' he said softly. Then, leaning close, he whispered, 'Do not be fearful. I believe every word you say.'

He took the girl as close to the saint as was safe, and then asked for a sword. The nearest guard offered his weapon, which Birbal took in his right hand. At once, another group of soldiers surrounded the saint's followers.

'So,' said Birbal, 'the child will speak first, and then the saint.'

With his left hand, Birbal took a handful of pistachios from his pocket and held them out for the saint.

'Would you like a salted almond?' he asked the blind man.

The saint's hand hovered a moment but then he shook his head. 'No, thank you,' he replied. 'I do not like salted almonds . . .'

Birbal nodded and turned back to the girl, pocketing the nuts. 'Go on, my child . . .'

The girl cleared her throat and began to tell her tale.

'I was in bed,' she said, 'when my mother began to scream that bandits had arrived on our farm. She grabbed me and ran to the water buffalo pen. There she hid me amongst the straw and dung and begged me to remain quiet. I sobbed and sobbed but it was no use. My mother turned and went to help my father, but it was already too late. This man took his sword and –'

Birbal held up his hand.

'How did he hold the sword, child?' he asked, to the bewilderment of everyone at court.

'I –' began the girl, but Birbal hushed her once again.

He held the sword with two hands and hefted it above his head. Then he turned to face the saint, whose breathing grew louder and faster.

'How did he bring it down, child?' Birbal asked again. 'Was it like this . . .?'

To horrified gasps, Birbal brought the sword downwards, its murderous arc ending right between the saint's eyes. But the saint saw it too, and threw himself aside, just before the blade struck home. The gasps grew louder, before turning into shouts and jeers. The blind saint could see.

'GUARDS!!!!' said Akbar. 'Arrest this murderer and his gang!'

Later, once the girl and her family had left and the bandit awaited his sentence in jail, Akbar asked Birbal how he had been so sure.

'What if the saint had been blind?' he asked. 'You would have killed him.'

'Yes,' said Birbal, 'and I would now be sitting in his place, awaiting my fate . . .'

'Were you not scared of being wrong?' asked Akbar.

'No,' said Birbal. 'Not when the girl was so adamant. She is only a child, Your Majesty. Why would she have remained so true to her story, even in your presence?'

'I see,' said Akbar.

'Besides,' Birbal added. 'It's amazing what one can learn from a handful of nuts . . .'

The Charmed Ring

One day, a rich merchant decided to teach his son a lesson. The boy, Navin, lived a comfortable life and wanted for nothing, but his father worried that Navin might grow up to become lazy.

'You must go and seek your own fortune,' he said.

'What have I done wrong, Father?' Navin asked.

'Nothing, boy,' the merchant replied. 'But you have always been given everything. Now, you must earn your way in life.'

'Very well,' said a hurt and confused Navin.

'I will give you three hundred rupees so you don't

starve,' said his father. 'But do not return until your fortune is made.'

Navin packed a few possessions, said his goodbyes and left.

On the road, he came across two goat herders quarrelling over a dog.

'Look at it,' said the first. 'It is useless!'

The mutt was thin and its coat threadbare, but Navin felt sorry for it. All it needed was food.

'We might as well throw it into a well,' said the second goat herder.

'No!' Navin yelled. 'Please don't kill him.'

The goat herders turned to Navin. 'Mind your own business, boy,' said the first.

'I'll buy him!' said Navin.

'Buy him?' asked the second, before smirking. 'Do you have one hundred rupees, boy?'

Navin nodded.

'Here,' he said, taking the money from his tunic.

The herders pocketed the money greedily. As Navin led the dog away, one of them chuckled.

'What a foolish young man!' he said.

In the next town, Navin came across a woman trying to drown her cat.

'What are you doing?' Navin asked.

'Mind your own business, boy!' the woman replied. 'This wretched thing is worthless!'

The poor creature was even more flea-bitten and skinny than the dog. But Navin did not care. 'Spare it,' he said. 'I will buy it from you.'

The woman let go, looking confused. The cat scampered away and hid in a rose bush.

'You want to *buy* that mangy thing?'

'Yes,' said Navin. 'I'll give you one hundred rupees.'

The shocked woman hastily agreed, grinning as Navin took the cat in his arms and left, the dog at his heels.

'What a senseless idiot,' she said, counting her money with glee.

Soon, Navin found yet another poor creature in need. The snake was long and thick, with ebony scales, and had been trapped by some villagers. They argued over the best way to kill it. Navin took pity at once, and threw himself across the trap.

'Take one hundred rupees for it!' he said. 'But, I beg you, don't kill this noble soul.'

The villagers were delighted to take the money. As Navin turned to go, with the snake over his shoulder, and the cat and dog at his feet, an old woman smiled. She watched the gleeful villagers taunting the boy and cursed them.

'One day,' she said, 'that boy will be blessed for his kindness.'

When evening fell, Navin found a cave for shelter. Penniless, and without food, he sat down and wept. 'I am a fool!' he lamented. 'What will I do now?'

In the morning, with no other choice, he returned to his father's house.

'You brainless wretch!' his father bellowed when he heard Navin's story.

'But, Father, I –'

'Go and sleep in the stables!' his father ordered. 'You shame your family! You will never enter my house again!'

So Navin lived in the stables, sleeping on a grass bed with the cattle. His new companions slept with him, the cat by his feet, the dog by his head, and the snake draped across him. They grew very fond of their master, and followed Navin wherever he went.

One night, as the others slept, the snake whispered to Navin.

'Master,' it said. 'I wasn't always a serpent.'

'What do you mean?' Navin asked.

'I am the son of a great rajah,' the snake replied. 'My father's name is Indrasha, and my kingdom is far away.'

'But how did you become a snake?'

'I was cursed by a wicked magician,' the snake replied.

'Where is your kingdom?' Navin asked.

'Do you know the great mountain?' asked the snake.

'Yes,' said Navin. 'Across the jungle, to the west.'

'That's it,' the snake replied. 'There is a sacred spring at the foot of the mountain. My father's country can be found by diving into that spring.'

'Very well,' said Navin. 'I will take you back to your family.'

'Thank you, kind master,' the snake hissed.

Navin shook his head.

'Don't thank me, friend,' he said. 'You are a creature of this earth, just like me. I am happy to help you.'

The snake wrapped itself round Navin and the two friends fell fast asleep.

At dawn, Navin jumped to his feet. 'Let's go quickly!' he said to the snake. 'Your father must miss you terribly.'

The snake was pleased. 'My father has many treasures,' he said. 'When we get back, I will ask him to give you some.'

'No, no,' Navin replied. 'I don't want rewards.'

'I know,' said the snake. 'That's why you deserve them!'

'But . . .'

'No,' said the snake. 'Your kindness to me cannot go unrewarded.'

Navin and his companions set off at once, travelling for many days, through forests and fields, and into the dense jungle at the foot of the mountain. When they arrived they were tired and hungry, but eager to find the snake's kingdom. But, at the sacred spring, the cat and the dog grew suddenly glum.

'Dear master,' the dog whined. 'We cannot swim very well. How will we come with you?'

'Yes,' said the cat. 'We cannot bear to lose you.'

'Don't worry,' Navin replied. 'I will be back soon. I won't abandon you.'

And, with that, the boy and the snake dived into the water.

Indrasha, the rajah, soon learnt of his son's return. But the snake refused to go to the palace until Navin was given his reward. When Indrasha came to find his son, the snake bowed its head.

'Dear Father,' he said. 'This boy saved my life. I am in his debt forever.'

'My son!' said Indrasha through tears of joy. 'Ask for anything, and I will give it. Without you, my son, riches mean nothing!'

'I ask for your ring, your pot and the spoon you stir the pot with.'

Indrasha nodded. 'Of course!' he declared. 'And I will give gold too!'

'Please, Your Majesty,' said Navin. 'I do not need anything.'

Indrasha hugged Navin to his chest.

'Nonsense!' he said. 'I am your servant forever. I can never repay your kindness in full.'

Navin agreed.

'But no gold,' he said. 'I am happy to take the ring, the pot and the spoon.'

'Fair enough,' the rajah replied. 'Please stay with us for a while.'

However, Navin refused. 'I will return one day,' he said. 'For now, I have two other friends to help.'

Navin and the snake returned to the sacred spring.

'I wish I could give you much more,' said the snake, as they said their farewells.

'You have given me more than enough,' Navin replied. 'Goodbye, brother, until we meet again.'

'The ring, the pot and the spoon are enchanted,' the snake revealed. 'They will make your life wonderful, my friend.'

As they embraced, the snake whispered instructions in Navin's ear. And then Navin dived into the cool, clear water.

On the other side, his friends jumped for joy when Navin emerged.

'Master!' they shouted. 'You have returned to us!'

'Yes,' said Navin.

Together they returned to Navin's father's house. There

Navin packed a few more belongings and then left again forever.

One morning, some weeks later, they found a riverbank between a mighty river and a glorious forested mountain. There, Navin took out his rewards. The snake had whispered instructions to Navin, which he now recalled. Firstly he spoke to the ring, and asked for somewhere to live. And instantly a magnificent bungalow appeared. Amazed and delighted, the cat and the dog followed Navin inside.

In the kitchen, they found a mahogany table. Navin removed the pot from his sack and put it down. Taking the spoon, he stirred the empty pot and asked for a pile of delicious food. The table was immediately laden with fruits and nuts, spiced rice pudding and sweetmeats, tender lamb and mountains of fragrant rice.

'Can this be real?' the cat asked.

On their long journey, Navin had kept the pot and spoon hidden, in case they were stolen. Instead, they had survived on scraps. Now they had a rajah's feast.

'Tastes real,' the dog said, after wolfing down some lamb.

'There's something else,' Navin told them.

Suddenly, a beautiful girl, with golden brown hair and eyes of pale honey, appeared. She smiled warmly.

'Hello,' she said. 'I am Gita and this is my house. Feel free to join me for dinner.'

*

Navin and Gita soon fell deeply in love, and eventually they were married. For seven long and wonderful years they lived blissfully by the river, their lives full of joy and laughter. Then, one morning, everything changed. Navin and his wife Gita were by the river when a sudden gust of wind blew down from the mountain. Gita was holding her favourite silk scarf, which floated away on the breeze, landing in the water. The current was strong and the violet scarf floated along for many miles, following the river into the neighbouring kingdom. There a lazy and selfish prince called Kunal found it.

Convinced the scarf was a blessing, Kunal rushed home with it. The scarf carried Gita's scent – honey and cream and spices – and Kunal grew enchanted. He demanded to know whose scarf it was, but in vain. He locked himself in his room and sulked for days. Refusing to eat or drink, and barely sleeping, Kunal grew depressed.

'This scarf is a sign!' he told everyone that asked. 'It belongs to my future wife and I will find her!'

Kunal's father, the rajah, grew irritated by his son's actions. Kunal was being foolish, and mocking his father's honour. Exasperated, the rajah turned to his aunt, who was a powerful and evil witch.

'Pah!' said the witch when she heard. 'Kunal is a weakling! I told you to strangle him at birth!'

'But he is my only son,' the rajah replied.

'You are young enough to have more sons,' the witch told him.

'Perhaps, dear aunt,' said the rajah. 'But Kunal is the only one, for now . . .'

'Very well,' said the witch. 'I will find this girl for him.'

She took the scarf from Kunal and inhaled Gita's scent. Then, transforming herself into a bee, she flew off. Her senses were sharp, and after a few days she found Gita. Dropping to the ground, she became a frail old woman, bent over in mock pain with a walking stick for support. When kind Gita saw her, she went to help at once.

'Dear child,' said the witch. 'My family have deserted me. I am homeless and hungry. Please help me . . .'

'Of course!' Gita cried. 'How terrible your children must be! Let me help you into the house.'

'Oh, thank you, girl,' the witch replied. 'If only my own daughters were as kind as you.'

When Navin returned from hunting with his faithful pets, Gita explained what had happened. Navin smiled.

'Dear woman,' he said. 'Of course you can stay. We are blessed with plenty and happy to share.'

'You are too kind,' said the witch, trying not to smile too.

The couple treated the witch as a mother. She wanted for nothing, her every need taken care of. As each day passed, the witch learnt more of Navin's enchanted possessions. One evening, she pulled Gita aside.

'Dear girl,' she began, 'my husband was just as loving

and noble as Navin. But then he died suddenly and left me with nothing.'

'How terrible,' Gita replied, growing tearful.

'I worry for your future, lovely Gita,' the witch continued. 'What if, God forbid, Navin should be killed whilst hunting? Your special ring would be lost, and you would be left all alone.'

Gita understood her meaning at once. The old woman was wise and caring, and Gita decided to tell Navin.

'Why didn't I think of this?' said Navin, when they spoke. 'How very foolish of me.'

Two days later, Navin woke early and went for a swim. The witch saw her chance and asked Gita if she could see the magical ring.

'Just for a moment,' she added.

Gita suspected nothing and agreed. But, as soon as the ring appeared, the witch snatched it from Gita's hand. In an instant, she transformed back to a bee and flew away. The cat and the dog could only watch and weep with their mistress.

Upon her return, the witch went straight to Kunal. The prince lay on his bed, groaning.

'Get up, you worthless rat!' she howled. 'Here is your ring!'

'But where is the girl?' the prince wailed. 'I *want* the girl!'

'The ring will bring her to you,' the witch explained. 'Now stop acting foolishly and show some honour!'

The witch explained the enchanted ring's powers and Kunal hurried outside. As soon as he'd spoken, the magnificent bungalow appeared in the palace gardens. Almost mad with desire, Kunal rushed inside. Gita, scared and bewildered, sat weeping on the floor.

'My love!' cried Kunal. 'I have dreamt of this day!'

Gita looked up, shaking her head. 'I am not your love,' she whispered. 'My husband is Navin. I will never be yours.'

Kunal grew angry.

'The ring, the bungalow and everything inside it now belong to me!' he shouted. 'That includes you!'

As the witch appeared, Gita began to understand what had happened. Saddened and angry, she turned to Kunal. 'Do what you like,' she told him. 'I will never accept you.'

'Nonsense!' Kunal declared. 'In a month from now, we shall be married. Until then, you will stay in this bungalow.'

'There is no escape,' the witch added, taking the ring and swallowing it. 'And no ring, either . . .'

Gita sobbed as they left, and prayed that Navin would find her.

When Navin emerged from the river, he fell to his knees in anguish. His beautiful Gita and their wonderful home had vanished. His faithful companions were all that remained. The dog lay crying and the cat paced in distress. Navin stood and stumbled towards them.

'What evil is this?' he asked.

The cat explained what had happened, and Navin felt his heart breaking.

'There is nothing left, then,' he replied.

'We couldn't stop the witch,' said the dog. 'We failed you.'

'But we will make it up,' the cat added. 'We will find Gita and the ring. I promise you!'

Navin nodded but said nothing. Instead, he went back to the riverbank, sat down and wept.

The cat and dog searched high and low for Gita. They followed the meandering curves of the mighty river, asking everyone they met for news. Then, some days into their quest, they came across a farmer's daughter in the neighbouring kingdom.

'The rajah's aunt,' she said, when the cat described the old woman who turned into a bee. 'She is an evil witch with dark powers. Everyone is afraid of her.'

'Did she return here?' asked the dog.

'Yes,' the girl replied. 'People say that a magnificent bungalow appeared in the palace grounds.'

'At last!' cried the cat.

They waited until dusk before creeping into the

palace grounds. The shadows were long and the guards failed to spot them. Soon they discovered their master's house, and inside was Gita, her face ashen, her eyes sore from tears.

'Mistress!' the dog said. 'We have come to rescue you!'

Though overjoyed to see them, Gita grew frightened. 'But what if the witch catches you?' she said.

'All we need is the ring,' the dog replied. 'Then we can escape.'

Gita shook her head in sadness. 'The ring is gone,' she whispered. 'The witch swallowed it. All is lost!'

'We will find a way!' said the dog.

Suddenly, the cat thought up a cunning plan. She pulled the dog to one side. 'Rats!' she whispered.

'What do you mean, dear friend?' the extremely puzzled dog asked.

The cat grinned. 'Come with me,' it said. 'I shall explain on the way.'

In the shadow of the palace wall, the cat explained its plan. It pointed out a large rat hole.

'See?' she said. 'I saw many rats as we entered the palace gardens.'

'Yes,' said the dog, 'but I still don't understand.'

'Just follow me,' the cat replied. 'Rats have a king. And where there is a rat king, there will be a rat prince . . .'

They crept down into the rats' nest. The tunnels were narrow and smelly, but soon they emerged on to a rock ledge, overlooking a huge cave. Below, hundreds of rats scurried about, in preparation for a great wedding. In the far corner, the Rat King sat and watched. At his side was his son, the Rat Prince.

'The prince is getting married,' said the cat. 'But imagine a wedding without the bridegroom . . .'

The cat took off suddenly. It crept round the ledge, before dropping to some rocks directly behind the Rat King and his son. It waited patiently for the king to move away, and then, with one swipe of its paws, grabbed the Rat Prince and jumped back up to the waiting dog.

'Hurry!' it mumbled, with the Rat Prince firmly wedged between its teeth.

They ran back to the opening, and across the palace gardens, until they reached the bungalow. Inside, they found a wooden box, into which they put the Rat Prince.

'Stay calm, brother rat,' the cat said. 'We will not harm you.'

When Gita saw them, she grew angry.

'Release that poor creature at once!' she said.

'I can't, mistress,' the cat replied. 'I have a plan. Don't worry, the box has air holes and I will bring him some food.'

'But why kidnap him?' Gita asked.

'Because now the Rat King will help us,' the cat explained. 'I had no choice . . .'

With the Rat Prince safe, the cat and the dog returned

to the palace walls. They found the Rat King searching for his son.

'Who would take my son so cruelly?' the Rat King cried. 'And on the eve of his wedding?'

The cat stepped from the shadows and purred. 'Why, it was I, Your Majesty,' it said.

As the other rats cowered in terror, the king stood firm. 'But why?' it asked. 'And why *boast* of your wickedness? You are unlike any cat I've ever met.'

'I do not wish to harm your son,' the cat replied. 'I only need a favour.'

The Rat King was baffled. 'But why not just ask?' it said.

'Because I'm a *cat*,' the moggy replied. 'Why would you listen to me? I usually *eat* rats . . .'

'Oh,' said the Rat King. 'Fair enough . . .'

The cat explained everything to the Rat King, before revealing its plan. The Rat King agreed at once, anxious to save his son.

'We will rescue your charmed ring,' said the Rat King. 'I promise on the life of my only son!'

'Yes,' said the cat. 'I *thought* you might . . .'

By midnight, the witch was soundly asleep. The Rat King's bravest warriors, having heard the plan, were ready. The first rat kept watch on the witch's windowsill. When he was certain she wouldn't wake up, he summoned his sister. She slid to the floor and weaved across the room, until she was under the bed. A third rat quickly joined her. This one climbed the sheets, until it reached the pillows. Taking a deep breath, it crept gingerly across the witch's face.

Slowly, deliberately, it pushed its tail deep into the witch's mouth and down her throat. Then it gave a sharp wiggle. The witch coughed, once, twice and then a third time. Suddenly the charmed ring erupted from her belly on a wave of vomit. The third rat leapt up, knocking the ring with its paw. The ring sailed through the air, towards the second rat, who caught it between her teeth. As the witch sat up and roared, the second rat flicked her jaws, and the ring sailed towards her brother, still balanced on the windowsill. He took the ring, and as the other two vanished behind the walls, he scurried away.

The witch ran to the door and threw it open. 'My ring, my ring!' she cried. 'They have taken my ring!'

As alarm bells rang, the cat and the dog received the enchanted ring and returned to the bungalow. Inside, the Rat King thanked Gita for taking such good care of his son.

'I would invite you to his wedding,' the Rat King said. 'But I fear we will have to find a new home. The witch will come after us, for sure.'

'Dear Rat King,' said Gita. 'Summon all of your subjects, quickly. We will take you all with us.'

The Rat King called to his guards, who drew tiny trumpets and blew on them. Suddenly every last rat scurried inside, until each room was teeming with rodents.

The cat and the dog were anxious to leave, and urged Gita to use the enchanted ring. Taking it from the cat, she whispered . . .

Navin sat by the river, certain that he would never again see his wife or his friends. He wondered where Gita was, and whether she was thinking of him. Suddenly he heard the barking of his faithful dog.

'Master, master!' the dog panted. 'We have the ring, but be quick! There is no time to lose . . .'

Navin sprang to his feet, his heart pounding with unbridled joy. Could it be true? The magnificent bungalow had reappeared, and standing at the door was Gita.

'Oh, my love, my life!' Navin cried, 'You have come back!'

'Hurry!' Gita urged him. 'We must leave this place before the witch comes looking for us!'

'But where will we go?' Navin asked.

'Anywhere,' Gita replied. 'Only far from *here*.'

As Navin stepped across the threshold, five small rats crawled up his legs and clung on to his tunic.

'Hello!' they squeaked.

'We have a few extra guests,' said Gita.

Navin smiled and took the ring from her. He imagined a place just like the one they were in. Somewhere with a mighty river, perhaps in a valley, bordered by ancient trees that rose into mountains. Then he asked the ring for his dream. The bungalow's door slammed shut and they were gone . . .

The Rabbit and the Lion

Once there lived a mean and boastful lion. Although he was already king of his domain, the lion was often very cruel. He wanted the other animals to fear him, and he bullied them every day.

'*Pah!*' he'd say. 'I am more noble than any of you!'

His poor younger brother, tired of the Lion King's bullying, decided to challenge him one day.

'The other animals don't respect you,' he said.

The Lion King chuckled.

'You're wrong!' he boasted. 'Of course they respect me. Look how they tremble when I approach them!'

'That is fear,' his little brother replied. 'It's not the same thing.'

'But . . .'

His brother shook his head.

'They are scared of you,' he said. 'But they don't like you. And why would they? You are mean and unfair.'

'Who cares?' said the Lion King. 'I am the strongest, the bravest and the most clever. Who can challenge me?'

'There's always someone stronger or cleverer,' his little brother warned. 'One day you might regret your pride . . .'

The Lion King ignored his younger brother's warning. Instead, he went for a walk round his kingdom. But eventually he grew concerned that his brother was right. Maybe the other animals didn't respect him. So he decided to ask some of them, and soon he came across a brown-coated jackal.

'You, jackal!' roared the Lion King. 'Tell me who is the strongest animal!'

The jackal began to tremble, but replied quickly. 'Why, you are, Your Majesty,' it said.

'And do you respect me . . .?'

The jackal wanted to tell the truth but was far too frightened. So he lied.

'Yes,' he whimpered. 'I respect you . . .'

Satisfied, the Lion King walked on. By a fallen tree, he found an ebony-scaled cobra, snoozing in the sunshine.

'Wake up, you slithering wretch!' the Lion King growled.

At once, the cobra sat up, ready to strike. But when it saw the Lion King, it grew worried.

'Tell me, sly snake,' said the Lion King. 'Do you respect me?'

'Why, of course,' the cobra hissed. 'You are the king.'

The lion smiled. 'And you're not lying because you're scared of me?'

'No, no,' the snake lied. 'I would never lie to you, mighty lion!'

The lion grinned and walked on. The next animal it met was a huge water buffalo drinking from a lake.

'Your Majesty!' the buffalo cried. 'Please don't hurt me!'

'No, no,' said the Lion King. 'I'm not hungry today, so you're perfectly safe. I just wanted to ask you something.'

'Anything,' the poor creature said, shuddering anxiously.

'Do you respect me?' asked the Lion King.

'Yes,' the water buffalo lied. 'You are mighty and noble, and king of the animals . . .'

'Excellent,' said the lion. 'Actually, I am a little bit hungry . . .'

And with that, the cruel Lion King pounced on the buffalo . . .

The following day, as the Lion King rested, his belly full of buffalo, a rabbit happened to hop past. The Lion King looked up.

'You!' he snapped. 'Come here at once!'

The rabbit leapt towards the lion, completely unafraid.

'Yes?' asked the rabbit.

'Do you respect me?'

The rabbit shrugged. 'No,' it said truthfully. 'Not really . . .'

The Lion King was confused. 'I'm sorry,' he replied. 'Did you say no?'

The rabbit nodded and the Lion King sat up. 'But you *are* frightened of me?'

'Not really,' the rabbit replied. 'I mean, you're scary but that doesn't bother me.'

The Lion King was enraged. He rose to his feet and growled. 'Why not?' he demanded. 'I am the greatest animal in the kingdom!'

The rabbit shook its head. 'No,' it said. 'There is someone greater than you!'

'What?' the lion roared, baring his sharp teeth. 'Who is greater than me?'

The rabbit smiled. 'I'll show you, if you like.'

The Lion King agreed, and set off after the rabbit. They walked past the lake and through the forest, until they reached a clearing. There, next to a deserted hut, was an old well.

'He's in there,' said the rabbit.

'Who?'

'The scariest, noblest and greatest animal in the

kingdom,' the rabbit replied. 'Be careful, though. He might eat you!'

The Lion King sneered with pride. 'You are very mistaken!' he said. 'No animal is a match for me!'

The Lion King leapt to the well and peered over the side. Then he gave his loudest and most fearful roar. But, instead of cowering in terror, the animal in the well simply growled back.

'*See?*' said the rabbit. 'He's not scared of you.'

The lion tried again, but this time the roar that came back was even louder.

'Is that another lion down there?' he asked the rabbit.

'Oh yes,' the rabbit said. 'He's very strong and much cleverer than you. He's the one I respect . . .'

The Lion King grew furious. 'We'll see about that!' he snarled. 'I will challenge him to a fight!'

And, with that, the lion jumped into the well. The rabbit sighed and shook its head.

'What a silly lion,' it said, hopping away.

The Cruel Crane

One day, a huge ivory crane flew over a shimmering lotus pond, which lay below a pear tree. Candy pink flowers floated on the water and beneath them swam many delicious fish. However, a long dry season had begun to evaporate the water in the pond, and its inhabitants faced great danger. Unless the monsoon rains came early, the fish would face certain death.

The crane, spotting an easy meal, settled on the branches of the pear tree.

'My, what tasty fish,' it said. 'I wonder how many I can eat?'

After watching the pond for a while, the crane flew down to the water's edge. When the fish saw him, they grew frightened. A few brave ones swam to the surface, but kept their distance.

'Go away, cruel crane,' the bravest fish said. 'We won't be your lunch today.'

The crane sighed. 'I would never take advantage of you,' it lied. 'Not when you are in danger.'

'What danger?' the fish asked.

'The sun is drying out your pond,' the crane said, pretending to be sad. 'Within days, the water will be gone and you will be dead.'

'Why do you care?' said the fish. 'You would eat us anyway.'

'Exactly,' the crane replied. 'But I don't want to eat rotten fish. If you die, I will go hungry. My only choice is to save you all, and take you somewhere safer. That way, I'll have a chance to catch a few of you, and you won't be putrid.'

The fish considered the crane's words. The pond *was* drying out. Perhaps it made sense to accept help from the crane?

'What if we accept your kind offer?' the fish asked.

The crane gave a smile. 'Why, brother fish, there's an enormous pond very close by. It's teeming with life. I will take you there.'

'But how will you do that?' asked the fish.

'In my beak, of course!' the crane replied.

'Pah!' the fish cried. 'You will just eat me!'

'No, no!' the crane protested. 'I swear you will be safe. Upon my honour!'

'Prove it,' the fish replied.

'Fair enough,' the crane agreed. 'Let me take one fish with me, to see the great pond. When I come back with your friend, you'll believe my word.'

The bravest fish took the crane's offer to the others. They discussed the situation for a while, and then agreed to accept help. When the crane heard their decision, it held back a sly grin.

'No time to lose,' it said, opening its beak. And into its mouth the bravest fish popped.

The crane soared away, and flew for a mile before landing at the great pond. It let the fish out, watching as it explored the waters.

'This is a wonderful place!' said the fish when it returned. 'Amazing. I can't wait to live here.'

'*See?*' said the crane. 'I am a bird of my word, brother fish.'

Back at home, the brave fish told the others what it had seen. Instantly, every fish grew eager to leave. The great pond sounded like heaven. When the crane heard the news, it nearly laughed out loud.

'Excellent,' it said. 'I'll take all of you, but one by one. There's only so much space in my beak.'

The brave fish went first, and the crane set off. Only this time it settled on a tree overlooking the pond.

'You silly little thing,' it sneered. 'Now, I believe it's my lunchtime.' He released the fish from its mouth and laid it on the wide branch.

Using its beak, it speared the fish and gobbled it up. All that remained were its bones, which fell to the ground. The crane smiled and flew back for more.

'Who's next?' it asked the other fish.

'Me, me, me!!!' came a chorus of voices . . .

And so, one by one, each fish went happily to its end. Soon the cruel crane was stuffed, and a huge pile of fish bones sat beneath the tree. But the crane had spied another creature whilst tricking the fish. It was a crusty old crab with giant black pincers. The cruel bird salivated at the thought of sweet crabmeat and flew back.

'Brother crab,' the crane called out on arrival. 'I have taken the fish to a great pond, full of water. Won't you join them?'

'I see,' the crab replied. 'I suppose I should leave too.'

'Then hurry,' said the crane. 'I am tired and this will be my last trip.'

The crab thought for a moment before replying. 'But I'm too big for your beak,' it said.

The crane nodded. 'Yes,' it said, feeling another pang of greed. 'You *are* quite large, aren't you?'

'Maybe I'll just stay here, then,' said the crab.

'No, no,' the crane replied. 'I'm sure there's a way to carry you.'

' I can think of one,' the crab replied. 'Why don't I hold on to your neck? My pincers are very strong . . .'

'Very well,' said the crane, looking forward to more feasting.

The crane bent down low and the crab took hold. Although its new passenger was heavy, the crane's wings were powerful, and away it went. As they approached the great pond, the crab spotted the mound of fish bones, and smiled to itself.

Ridiculous crane, it thought. *As if I'm as brainless as those fish.*

As the crane circled, the crab spoke up. 'Why are we circling this great tree?' it asked. 'The pond is just there . . .'

The crane cackled in delight. 'Because you have been fooled!' it boasted.

It swooped down to the branch.

'Now, loosen your grip,' the crane demanded.

'Hmmmm . . .' the crab replied. 'Maybe not.'

The crane sighed. 'Look,' it said. 'You have been outwitted. Now let go . . .'

'I think you might be confused,' the crab told the crane. 'Who tricked who this time?'

Suddenly, the crab tightened its grip, and the crane grew scared.

'I'm sorry, dear crab!' it cried. 'Please forgive me and I will take you down to the pond!'

The crab smiled. 'That seems fair,' it said. 'But hurry, otherwise I might get angry.'

The terrified crane flew down to the pond's edge and settled in the mud.

'There, brother crab!' it said. 'Now, let go!'

But the crab didn't listen. With a sharp snip, it cut through the cruel crane's neck, and the devious bird fell dead.

'Oops!' said the crab, before sliding into the cool, clear water of its new home.

The Curious Good Fortune of
Harisarman the Hapless

Once there lived a hapless and unremarkable man called Harisarman. His life was filled with bad luck, failure and misery. When other men were starting families and making fortunes, Harisarman found himself without work and often insulted by his own wife.

'Useless man!' she would frequently say. 'What did I do wrong, to end up with you? Were my stars so ill-fated?'

Whilst his wife worked day and night to make ends meet, Harisarman just sat in their hut, complaining about how awful his life had become. Even as a child, he had been unfortunate. Smaller and weaker than the other boys in his village, he couldn't even run properly. Instead, Harisarman resembled a toad when he ran, and his own father would call him '*Frog*' and chuckle hurtfully.

The people of his village showed Harisarman little respect, teasing and insulting him. The old women would scowl and shoo him away, and in children's games he was always the joke. Indeed, some children had even created a rhyme with which to dishonour him.

> '*Harisarman the Lazy, Harisarman the Fool,*
> *Harisarman the dim-witted and useless old tool.*'

But one day, thanks to a curious run of good fortune, Harisarman's life began to change . . .

Realizing that the people in his village would never help him, Harisarman left. He walked to a nearby city, hoping to find work. He wandered the streets telling anyone he met of his awful life. With no jobs to be found, he decided to start begging. A passing merchant heard his desperate pleas and introduced himself.

'My name is Datta,' he said. 'I am a wealthy man, and I need a servant couple. If you have a wife, I can give you work and a place to live.'

'Oh, kind sir!' Harisarman cried. 'You have saved me!'

He fell to his knees and touched Datta's feet, a sign of respect. 'May you live for a thousand years!' he said.

'Yes, yes,' said Datta. 'Bring your wife to my house in the morning. I will be waiting.'

When Harisarman asked where the merchant lived, Datta pointed out the grandest house in the city, sitting high on a hill and surrounded by beautiful gardens. Thanking Datta once more, Harisarman hurried home in excitement.

'Woman, woman!' he yelled on arrival. 'Come quickly – I have secured our future!'

His wife, unaccustomed to seeing her wretched husband so happy, asked why he was shouting.

'I have found work in the city,' he explained. 'A wealthy merchant has asked me to become his servant.'

'A merchant?'

'Yes!' Harisarman replied. 'And he is rich, dear wife – as rich as can be! We are saved!'

And so Harisarman and his wife left their village and began a new life in the city. The work was hard but it paid well, and Harisarman's wife grew cheerful at the change in their fortunes.

'Perhaps now,' she said one evening, 'we can be like ordinary folk. We have money and food, and our future is secure. We could even have children . . .'

Datta was very satisfied with Harisarman and his wife. They were very loyal and worked hard, and with good humour. Harisarman was content at last. As weeks became months, and months became years, his wife gave birth to two children, much to Harisarman's joy. Soon he was made head servant, and his pride began to grow.

Yet, despite all of this, Harisarman still felt unfulfilled. Even though he was working and had raised a family, he remained a servant. Datta provided work and food, and shelter and wages, but he had little respect for Harisarman. Then, on the wedding day of Datta's daughter, Harisarman learnt a lesson about his true standing in life.

Having planned and prepared a great feast for the numerous guests, Harisarman sat with his wife and their two young sons. Exhausted and hungry, he talked excitedly of the wonderful fare they would scoff that day. 'How blessed we are!' he said to his wife. 'Tonight we shall gorge on tender lamb and tandoor-roasted chicken, saffron-infused rice and delicious curry!'

But when evening arrived, and the noble guests had eaten and drunk until they collapsed, Harisarman and his family were forgotten. As he wearily cleared the mess left behind, his master's wife approached.

'Well done,' said his mistress. 'The guests were delighted with our efforts. Make sure to keep any untouched food, and tomorrow we shall feast once more.'

'Yes, mistress,' Harisarman replied. 'I will take some for my own family, if you would let me?'

His mistress smiled. 'Yes, yes,' she replied, waving her hand. 'There are plenty of leftovers on the dirty plates. Scrape off anything you like and enjoy it with my blessing . . .'

As she strode away, Harisarman felt his anger grow. Were his family so lowly, that they should eat unclean food? Sinking to his knees, a familiar depression took hold of Harisarman, and he wept.

Later, when he returned to his family, his wife was excited to see what wonderful food he had brought them. But when Harisarman shook his head and explained, she grew puzzled.

'But I thought . . .' she began.

'Today, I have learnt my true status,' he said with sorrow. 'I was foolish to think Datta and his wife would treat us as equals. We work hard and obey their every wish, yet to them we are nothing but animals. Is this our only destiny?'

For two more days, Harisarman brooded. Then, on the third, he had a splendid idea. That night, he told his wife. 'I am stupid and poor, and have never shown any ambition,' he said. 'That is why people disrespect me. But no more!'

'What will you do?' his wife asked, growing anxious.

'I will gain my master's respect,' Harisarman replied. 'But to achieve this, I need your help . . .'

He whispered his plan, and his wife's eyes grew wide in surprise.

The following evening, an important nobleman came to stay. Harisarman said nothing, and carried out his duties as usual. As Datta's noble guests ate and drank, Harisarman stood patiently, watching everything. Soon everyone went to bed, and Harisarman saw his chance. Sure that they slept, he crept softly from the house. Taking a lamp, he went to his master's stables, where the nobleman had tethered his magnificent horse. Harisarman quickly untied the great creature and rode off into the night. On the outskirts of the city, he found an abandoned yard, and there he hid the horse, before returning at speed so that he would not get caught.

When the sun rose next morning, Harisarman was already awake. Taking his wife aside, he whispered, 'There will be lots of fuss this morning. I won't say any more, in case my plan goes wrong, but please remember what I said.'

'When our master asks,' said Harisarman's wife, 'I must tell him that you are gifted.'

'Yes,' said Harisarman.

'But what if it doesn't work?' she asked.

'It will,' Harisarman told her. 'Trust me.'

When news of the missing horse reached Datta and his wife, they were furious. They called for the stable hands and grew angry with them.

'Go and find the horse at once!' Datta ordered.

'We cannot be embarrassed like this,' Datta's wife added. 'We will lose all respect if the horse isn't found!'

The stable hands left at once, and were gone all morning. When they returned empty-handed, Datta and his wife were sick with worry. Harisarman watched silently, waiting for the perfect moment. When Datta called every servant to the kitchens, to discuss the matter in secret, Harisarman called to his wife.

'Come quickly, my love.'

Datta raged and shouted but it did no good. The horse was gone, and soon the nobleman would discover it missing too. Harisarman cleared his throat. 'Master,' he said. 'I have a gift, which might help us.'

'A gift?' Datta asked.

'Yes,' Harisarman replied. 'Since childhood, I have been able to read the stars and do certain acts of magic.'

'Preposterous!' said Datta. 'You've never mentioned this before.'

Harisarman's wife spoke up. 'My husband is indeed a wise man,' she said. 'He might be able to help you, master.'

Datta and his wife, desperate to save their honour, agreed.

'Yesterday, my family were allowed only scraps from used plates,' Harisarman said. 'Yet today, you need my skills.'

Datta's wife grew ashamed and lowered her eyes.

'Dear Harisarman,' she pleaded. 'Please forgive my shameful act yesterday. If you can help us, I promise to show you the respect you deserve.'

Harisarman nodded. 'Very well,' he replied. 'But I must have complete privacy. Otherwise my gifts won't work.'

Harisarman locked himself away with paper and pencils, and began to draw. He drew circles and stars, and stick-images of animals, and wrote a few words here and there. None of it made sense, but that didn't matter. Harisarman's plan was working perfectly.

Some while later, he emerged from his room, carrying his diagram with him.

'There is an abandoned yard, east of the city,' Harisarman proclaimed. 'There, the thieves have hidden the horse. You'll have to be quick, master, because they will move it tonight.'

Datta set off at once, taking some men with him. He returned barely an hour later with the nobleman's horse.

'Oh, Harisarman!' he said. 'Today you have saved my family's honour. From this day forth, you will have a fine apartment and be paid double what you earn now!'

And so Harisarman grew richer and happier, and his family lived a fine life.

All was well, until the day came when Harisarman's gifts were needed again. The rajah was a close friend of Datta's, and one day he asked his friend's advice. For weeks, gold and jewels had been taken from the rajah's palace, but no thief had been caught.

'Dear friend,' the rajah said to Datta, 'What can I do? My palace should be safe and secure. What will people think of me, if they discover that my belongings are stolen so easily?'

Datta at once thought of Harisarman's gifts. 'Dear Rajah,' he said, 'I have the answer – my head servant, Harisarman. He is gifted and will discover your thief!'

Harisarman was immediately summoned to the palace. When he found out why, his knees began to tremble. Anxious and ashamed, Harisarman cursed his foolish lies. Now his secret would be exposed and the rajah would have him thrown in jail, or worse.

'My gifts don't work this way,' he said, attempting to cover his tracks. 'They don't just appear. I will require both time and privacy to solve this puzzle.'

On hearing this, the rajah had a room prepared for Harisarman. 'You shall have anything you need,' he said. 'But I beg you, oh wise sage, find me my thief!'

Placed in the guarded room, Harisarman wept. He thought of the shame his wife and children would suffer. Once his dishonesty was revealed, he would face terrible consequences. As he sat crying, however, his curious good fortune continued. Unseen by Harisarman, a maid called Jihva quietly entered the chamber. As she began to clean,

Harisarman cursed his lying tongue, completely ignorant of the maid's presence.

'Oh, deceitful *Tongue*!' he said, 'What terrible lies you have told because of greed. Oh, wicked *Tongue*, soon you will pay for your crimes!'

When Jihva heard Harisarman's words, she fell to her knees before him.

'Oh, gifted sage!' she cried, 'I beg mercy! You have caught me. I stole those things, with my brother!'

Harisarman, shocked and surprised, asked the woman her name.

'Why, it is Jihva,' said the maid, 'Just as you said.'

Harisarman smiled and shook his head in disbelief. The maid's name, Jihva, meant *tongue*! He was saved yet again.

'GUARD!' he bellowed. 'I have found the thief! Send for the rajah.'

Harisarman was rewarded with a large house and bags of gold. Once penniless and ridiculed, he was now a very wealthy man. Oh, how he wished that his old neighbours might see him now. Happy and relaxed, Harisarman hurried home to tell his wife the wonderful news. No longer would they work as servants. Now they were rich and had a house of their own. Life was finally perfect.

But there remained one more problem for Harisarman. The prime minister of the kingdom was called Devaj. He grew jealous of Harisarman's new wealth and status.

He found Harisarman's old village, and went there to find out about his past. As he spoke to Harisarman's old neighbours, Devaj's suspicions grew. On his return to the palace, he rushed to find the rajah.

'Your Majesty,' Devaj said. 'I am certain that Harisarman is a fraud. I went to his village, and none of his old neighbours believe his tale. They say he was penniless and dim-witted when he left for the city. They have never heard of his magic.'

'Yet he proved himself,' the rajah replied. 'Where you and your fellow advisors failed, this man succeeded. I will not allow you to dishonour him!'

'But, sir,' Devaj pleaded. 'He has no education and can barely read. How, then, could he study books of magic and astrology?'

Gradually, Devaj fed the rajah's suspicions, day after day, until shortly the rajah's patience snapped.

'Very well then!' the rajah bellowed. 'Send for Harisarman. I will set him a new challenge!'

When Harisarman arrived, baffled and nervous, he stood before the entire court.

'Your Majesty?' he enquired.

'My prime minister, Devaj, has called you a fraud,' the rajah said. 'So to help you prove your innocence, I have devised a new test.'

Harisarman felt his palms grow sticky and his heart start to flutter. Was he so close to being unmasked?

'But this gift is not like a well,' he replied. 'You can't just draw water when you like. My gifts are precious.'

'*Pah!*' cried Devaj, to murmurs from the court. 'He makes excuses because he's a liar!'

'I'm sorry, dear sage,' the rajah said. 'Your honour is being questioned. And because I have supported you, my honour is at stake too.'

'But I . . .' began Harisarman.

'You have no choice,' the rajah told him. 'You must complete the challenge or face the consequences.'

The rajah's groom came forward with a covered jug.

'I have hidden something inside this pitcher,' explained the rajah. 'To prove your gifts, you must tell me what it is.'

Frightened and distressed, Harisarman fell to his knees. What now for his wife and his two fine children? He recalled his childhood, and how people had taunted him. The shame his own father had felt, because Harisarman had been a whingeing and worthless failure. Had they all been right when they disrespected him? He remembered the nickname his father had given him, and he cried out.

'Oh, brainless Frog!' he wailed. 'How wretched your life has been, you who could never run properly!'

The rajah was astonished. He rose and kicked the pitcher over.

'There!' he cried.

As applause erupted all around court, Harisarman opened an eye. And there, amongst the broken clay fragments sat a frog. It croaked just once before hopping away.

'Oh, great wise man!' said the rajah. 'Your honour is saved! No one must ever doubt you again. Anyone who challenges you will pay! You are truly gifted.'

As Harisarman basked in yet another wonderful twist of fate, the rajah sacked his prime minister.

'Harisarman,' the rajah declared. 'You shall be my first minister. And all land, property and money Devaj had is now yours!'

So Harisarman the hapless and dim-witted fool, prospered for the rest of his life. And each night, as he relaxed in his own palace, having eaten the finest food, he thanked the stars for his most curious good fortune.

The Farmer and the Giant

One afternoon, a farmer called Lal Ram was digging a hole. Suddenly his spade hit something solid with a loud thud. Peering down, Lal spotted an earthen jar. He knelt to pull the jar from the ground, and saw that it had been sealed. Curious, he gave it a shake, but heard nothing inside. He set it aside and continued his task.

Later, as he was lying in bed, he began to wonder about the jar again. Perhaps it held something magical, he thought. Or, better still, something very precious? Lal got dressed and went out to his yard, where the jar sat by a well. Lal picked it up and studied it carefully. It was made of brown clay and someone had taken great care to seal the opening. Taking a knife, he began to prise it open.

Suddenly, a cloud of white smoke escaped the jar and rose upwards into the humid air. The smoke swirled in a cyclone, faster and faster until Lal saw a flash of green light. He fell backwards, landing on his behind, and gasped. Standing before him was a giant . . .

'MASTER!!!!' the giant bellowed. 'You have released me and now I am your slave!'

Lal scrambled away in shock. The giant wore an evil grin and clothes made of fine silk. On his head was a scarlet turban, and his ears were heavy with golden rings.

'Don't hurt me, oh mighty demon!' Lal cried.

'I WILL NOT HURT YOU!' the giant replied. 'I MUST SERVE YOU!'

Lal was confused. 'You will serve me?' he asked.

'YES!' the giant replied. 'ASK ME TO COMPLETE ANY TASK AND I WILL OBEY!'

Lal stood and dusted off his clothes. He edged closer to the giant, amazed and more curious than ever.

'What if I ask you to lower your voice?' he asked.

'Done,' said the giant. 'What else?'

'Draw me a bucket of water from the well,' said Lal.

Within seconds, the giant did as asked.

'Can it be true?' asked Lal. 'Have I really been so fortunate?'

The giant began to laugh. 'You have,' he eventually said. 'But you must agree to one condition.'

Lal nodded. 'What is it?' he asked.

'You must keep me busy,' the giant explained. 'When I am busy, I do not get hungry.'

'What happens if you get hungry?' asked Lal.

'Then I eat people,' the giant told him.

Lal shuddered at the thought but did not run. He had a large farm and there were many tasks the giant might do.

'I understand,' said Lal. 'Now, let me get some sleep and we'll continue in the morning.'

But the giant shook his head.

'No,' he replied. 'You must keep me busy at all times . . .'

'But it's dark,' said Lal, 'and I'm tired.'

'YOU MUST KEEP ME BUSY!' the giant hollered.

Lal sighed and asked the giant to tidy his yard. The giant lunged to the left in a flash, and then to the right. All around Lal, his yard grew tidier and within minutes the giant had finished.

'Done,' said the giant. 'Another task . . .'

Lal groaned. 'Fetch me ten more buckets of water,' he said.

Again, the giant completed the job in minutes. Lal shook his head and began to wonder if his fortune was really so great.

'I must sleep,' he moaned. 'Can't you take a rest?'

'No, master,' the giant replied. 'If I rest, I grow hungry. And then I must eat you . . .'

Lal began to think up more tasks for the giant, but each one was completed far too quickly. Soon Lal grew so exhausted that his eyelids drooped and his legs felt like jelly. Yet still the giant demanded more tasks.

'My land is full of rocks and stones,' Lal said through a yawn. 'Sift every grain of soil and remove them.'

The giant nodded and off he went. Lal was confident that the latest task would take much longer. He dropped to the ground and fell fast asleep. However, the giant returned just twenty minutes later and woke Lal up.

'It is done!' he proclaimed. 'Give me another job!'

Lal shook his head in sorrow. Rather than being a gift, the giant had become a curse. Soon he would run out of jobs to do and devour him. Lal sat down and wondered how to save himself. After a few minutes, he had an idea.

'I could do with a new house,' he told the giant. 'But it must be made of newly-cut timber from the rarest of trees.'

'Of course!' said the giant. 'Anything else?'

Lal began to imagine every room, and described them slowly. The giant listened carefully to every detail.

'This may take a while,' he said when Lal was finished.

'No problem,' the farmer replied in relief. 'Take your time.'

But barely an hour later, Lal's magnificent new house

was ready, and the giant was bored again. Growing desperate, Lal suddenly thought of something else. Something far cleverer . . .

'So,' he said to the giant. 'You must do anything I ask?'

'Yes,' said the giant.

'And I must make sure you're always busy?'

'Yes, master.'

'Or you will eat me?'

'I'm afraid so, master,' the giant replied.

Lal nodded and pointed to the field behind his brand-new house. 'I want you to create a stone pillar, at least a hundred feet tall,' he said.

'No problem,' the giant replied.

'Wait!' Lal ordered. 'There's more. Once the pillar is ready, I want you to climb it.'

'As you wish.'

'Then,' Lal added, 'when you reach the top, you must climb down again . . .'

The giant nodded. It sounded very straightforward, and he was certain to complete the task quickly.

'What happens when I climb down?' he asked his master.

Lal smiled. 'Once you get down, you will climb up again. You will continue to climb up and down until I tell you to stop.'

The giant agreed.

'It's a very odd request,' he said. 'But I must do as you ask . . .'

The giant whooshed off to a stone quarry and very quickly the pillar was hewn from solid rock. He picked it up and flew back to Lal's farm. There he secured the pillar in the field, and began to climb up and down at great speed. Lal stood at the bottom and applauded the giant.

'Well done!' he shouted. 'Now just keep going!'

As the giant climbed up and down, up and down, Lal began to chuckle.

'When do I stop, master?' the giant eventually asked.

'Oh, don't worry,' replied Lal. 'Just keep going and I'll let you know when . . .'

Lal chuckled and went off to his magnificent new house to get some sleep.

The Farmer and the Moneylender

When Kishan's father passed away, he was left with nothing but a plot of land. He had no cows, no water buffalo, and no ploughs or spades. Kishan was clever and strong, but had no way of growing any crops. His only choice was to sell his ancestral land and become a beggar.

One day, a devious moneylender arrived in Kishan's village. The man, Nilesh, told people he would give them loans. Desperate, Kishan went to see him, and explained his clever ideas. Nilesh was taken by the boy's plans and gave him the money he needed immediately.

Kishan bought ploughs and two water buffalo, seed and much more, and soon began to reap the rewards. After his first golden harvest, the wily Nilesh returned and heard of Kishan's good fortune.

'Your harvest has been generous,' Nilesh said. 'I will have to have a bigger repayment.'

Kishan, eager to start on his next crop, agreed without complaint and paid Nilesh more money. But the second crop was much harder work, and the weather played tricks on Kishan. When he needed sunshine, it would rain, and when he needed water, the sun would shine for weeks on end. When a long drought struck harvest time, Kishan's crops were almost ruined.

Nilesh returned soon afterwards, ready for his next payment. When he asked Kishan for his money, the boy looked glum.

'My harvest has failed, so may I pay less?' he asked.

'No, no,' said Nilesh. 'You will pay exactly what you owe . . .'

'But last harvest, you took more,' Kishan reminded him.

'Times change,' said Nilesh. 'Now, where is my money?'

The dry weather continued and each harvest was worse than the last. However, Nilesh returned for his money regardless. Soon Kishan was penniless and desperate once more, but Nilesh did not care. Eventually Kishan lost everything but a few rupees and the clothes on his back. Sad and angry, and determined to find a way to rebuild his fortune, Kishan went to see the moneylender again.

'You have taken everything I own,' he said. 'But you can't squeeze blood from a stone, sir. I have nothing left to give you.'

Nilesh, who had grown rich from the misery of other people, grinned. 'I only took what you owed,' he replied. 'No more, no less. In life, some people win and others lose . . .'

'Well, now that I've lost,' Kishan replied, 'perhaps you would tell me the secret to your riches?'

The moneylender laughed. 'Perhaps the mighty god, Ram, gave it to me?' he replied, his tone sarcastic and mocking. 'Maybe you should ask him!'

Even though Kishan knew the moneylender was teasing him, he had nothing to lose, and so he decided to find Ram. Using his last rupees to buy food for his journey, he packed his few belongings and set off.

Kishan walked all day long, until he met a Brahmin on the road.

'Dear priest,' said Kishan. 'If you could point the way to Lord Ram, I would be forever in your debt.'

He offered the Brahmin a rice cake. The priest eagerly accepted and wolfed it down. Then, without a word, he walked away, leaving Kishan confused and surprised.

Further on, he came across a wise man sitting by a spring.

'Oh, wise man,' said Kishan. 'You must have great knowledge. Please tell me where I can find Lord Ram.'

The wise man did not reply until Kishan gave him a mango.

'Why, how kind of you,' the wise man replied. 'This is delicious.'

'And what of Lord Ram?' Kishan asked again, making the man grin.

'You can't just *find* Lord Ram,' he explained in amusement. 'Why would I have travelled for many years, if Lord Ram was *easy* to find? Are you a fool?'

'No,' said Kishan. 'I am just a simple farmer seeking answers.'

'There is another beggar just like you,' said the wise man. 'He's sitting under a banyan tree, further down this road. Like you, he's awaiting a miracle – you'd make good friends.'

The wise man bellowed in laughter and dismissed Kishan with a wave of his hand.

'Idiot!' he called out as Kishan walked on.

After another hour, Kishan found the banyan tree. Taking shelter beneath it was the beggar. He wore a ragged cloak and was shoeless and dirty. Kishan sat beside him and unwrapped the last of his food.

'My belly aches with hunger,' the beggar said. 'Perhaps I could have some of your food?'

Though Kishan's own belly grumbled, he realized that the beggar was far hungrier.

'I am young and strong,' said Kishan. 'Here, sir, take it all.'

He offered the coconut dosa pancake – the last of his provisions.

'But you have nothing left,' said the beggar. 'Why give it to me?'

Kishan gave a weary smile.

'Because you asked,' he replied. 'And your need is greater than mine.'

The beggar nodded and took a bite. 'How delicious,' he said. 'Where are you going, friend?'

Kishan sat back and told his tale, and the beggar listened keenly.

'Do you know where I may find Lord Ram?' he finally asked.

'Oh yes!' said the beggar with a grin wider than the River Ganges. 'I know *exactly* where Lord Ram is.'

'Where, oh where?' Kishan cried, standing up to look around him.

'Why, he sits under a banyan tree, eating coconut dosa!'

Suddenly the beggar's rags were transformed. There, before Kishan, sat Lord Ram in fine silken robes. He wore a golden crown, and held his golden bow. A garland of crimson roses hung round his neck.

'Oh, mighty Lord Ram!' said Kishan, falling to his knees.

'Stand up, boy,' Ram replied, 'and tell me what you want of me.'

'Only your blessing,' said Kishan. 'I wish to rebuild my life.'

Ram reached into his garments and produced a conch shell.

'Take this conch,' said Ram. 'Blow into it and you will have whatever you wish. But you and only you will be able to use it.'

'Oh, mighty Ram!' said Kishan. 'Surely I should pass some test before you bless me with this gift?'

When Ram smiled, the birds broke into song and previously wilted flowers sprang into bloom. He held up the pancake and took another bite.

'I was hungry and you gave me your last crumbs,' Ram reminded him. 'Now, your kindness is repaid. But be wary of tricksters, boy. The greed of some people knows no end . . .'

And with that, Lord Ram melted away into a sapphire mist and was gone.

Kishan returned to his village, and set about rebuilding his fortune. He bought back his father's land and planted new crops, but always stayed honest, never taking advantage of the conch's power. Each evening, he slept peacefully, knowing that he had been very fortunate. He had more than enough and his life was wonderful.

However, Nilesh the moneylender soon heard of Kishan's return. When he saw how the boy had prospered, he grew envious. And when he offered Kishan more loans, the boy refused. Shocked, furious and full of jealousy, Nilesh vowed he would bankrupt Kishan a second time.

He must have some help, thought Nilesh. *How else did he grow so rich so quickly?*

Nilesh decided to spy on Kishan and discover his secrets. He watched from behind a large hibiscus bush, for days on end. Then, one evening, he saw Kishan blow into the conch. And at once a brand-new plough appeared.

What a treasure that is! the astounded moneylender thought. *I must make it mine!*

The next day, as Kishan toiled in his fields, Nilesh stole into his house and took the magical conch. He hurried home and wondered what he should ask for. As he was unmarried and lonely, he decided to ask for a beautiful wife. He held the conch to his lips and blew into it. But nothing happened. No matter how hard he tried, the conch would not make a sound. After many failed attempts, he gave up, throwing the shell to the floor in disgust.

The following morning, Nilesh decided to offer Kishan a pact.

'Look,' he said, when he found him. 'I have stolen your conch.'

'Thief!' Kishan yelled.

'Be quiet!' Nilesh ordered. 'If you want it back, you will listen.'

Kishan lowered his voice.

'Why should I care what you say?' he asked.

'Because unless you do, I will destroy the conch,' said Nilesh, smirking at his own guile. 'Then no one can use it.'

'But the conch is mine,' Kishan replied. 'Why should I share it?'

Nilesh smirked again. 'It's just good business,' he said. 'Without the conch, you are lost. But if we share it, we can both make money . . .'

When Kishan failed to reply, Nilesh continued, 'I have the conch but can't use it. You can use it, but don't have it. Unless we share, it is useless . . .'

Never greedy, Kishan considered Nilesh's deal and eventually agreed. 'I suppose it makes sense,' he replied.

Nilesh gave a sly smile, delighted that his scheme had worked. 'I promise to return your conch,' he said. 'But you must agree to my terms.'

'Explain your offer,' said Kishan.

'For everything you gain, I must get double,' said Nilesh. 'So if you have one chicken, I get two and so on . . .'

'Double?'

'Yes,' said Nilesh. 'Do we have a deal?'

Kishan reluctantly agreed.

For a year, Kishan stuck to the bargain. Even though Nilesh had cheated him, Kishan was very well off. He began to help the other villagers, and they grew wealthy too. But Nilesh had far, far more than everyone else, and his greed had no limit. Then, one summer, Kishan forgot to ask the conch for fair weather and a great drought destroyed all the crops.

In serious trouble, Kishan blew into the conch and a well appeared on his land. But when he saw the hardship of his neighbours, Kishan grew guilty, and shared his water with some of them. Nilesh, however, had gained two new wells. Through greed, he began to charge the villagers for water, and so his wealth grew as others suffered.

Kishan was so enraged by Nilesh's greed that he sat for days, thinking of a way to stop the avaricious moneylender. Eventually, he came up with a plan. He took the conch and hoisted it to his mouth.

'Oh, mighty Lord Ram,' he said, 'you warned me against tricksters but I didn't heed your words. Now, I wish to make things right. Take my left eye, I beg you . . .!'

Instantly, Kishan's left eye fell into shadow. Across the village, Nilesh was proudly admiring his land and wells. Suddenly, both of his eyes failed and he fell blind.

'*Arrggghhhh!!!!*' he cried. 'What evil is this?'

In shock and confusion, Nilesh tripped over a brand-new plough. He tumbled into one of his wells and drowned.

To thank Kishan for saving them from the moneylender, the villagers came to his aid. And despite his blindness, Kishan went on to live a long and prosperous life, happily sharing his fortune with his neighbours.

The Magic Bowl

On the day that his grandfather passed away, Suraj was just fourteen years old. Already orphaned, the loss of his grandfather left Suraj all alone in the world. Penniless and hungry, he had nowhere to turn. He spent those first lonely weeks begging for food and work around his village, but soon the villagers chased him away. He fled home in tears, feeling desperate and lost.

Then two days before Diwali, the festival of lights, Suraj decided to visit the goddess Parvati's temple and ask for her blessing. The journey was difficult and Suraj had no food or shoes, and only a small pot of water. He arrived tired and hungry, his feet aching. At the temple doors, he collapsed and fell fast asleep. He slept for an hour until a gentle nudge woke him up.

'Do not sleep here,' said a kind-faced woman. 'Come inside and eat something. You look terrible, my son.'

Suraj stood and dusted off his ragged clothing. 'I can't enter,' he said. 'The goddess will be angry because I am unclean.'

The woman smiled. Her hair was jet-black, and her caramel eyes and skin shone. 'Let me worry about Parvati,' she replied. 'Now, hurry up!'

The temple was deserted, despite the piles of saffron rice and sweetmeats that lay around. A huge statue of Parvati stood in the centre, garlanded with marigolds.

'Eat, eat!' the woman urged, as she poured water from a brass jug.

Suraj ate greedily, and soon he was feeling much better. As he drank from his cup, the woman whispered gently, 'Now, why did you come to see me?' Suraj rubbed his eyes in disbelief. The kind woman *was* the goddess Parvati. As he watched in astonishment, her old rags turned into fine silks and a crown of gold appeared on her head. He fell to her feet at once.

'Mighty Parvati!' he wept. 'Please forgive me. If I had known it was you, I –'

'Stop crying,' Parvati replied. 'You are very welcome here. Please tell me your troubles, son.'

Suraj kept his head bowed as he explained his story. When he was finished, he looked up and saw Parvati in tears.

'How wretched your life has been,' the goddess said. 'Here, take this magic bowl and you will never starve again.'

Suraj took the simple wooden vessel and stood.

'Thank you,' he said. 'I am very grateful to you.'

'May you stay blessed, poor Suraj,' Parvati replied.

Suraj departed after the festival and returned to his village. There, although still poor, he was no longer hungry. The bowl provided every meal Suraj asked for, and he was contented. However, he also grew guilty. Although he had plenty, many of his fellow villagers were starving. So one evening, Suraj asked for a mighty feast to feed them all. The people were very grateful but they soon told others of Suraj's special bowl. The gossip spread across the kingdom, and Suraj became very popular.

Before long, news of the magic bowl reached the rajah. He grew curious and summoned his advisors.

'Find out where this boy lives,' he demanded. 'I want to visit him.'

Two days later, the rajah rode to Suraj's village with two of his guards. When he found Suraj's hut, he was shocked to see so many people waiting. Inside, he found the boy feeding many more villagers.

'Your Majesty!' said Suraj, before giving a bow.

'This bowl must have great magic,' the rajah replied. 'I want you to bring it to the palace. I am throwing a great feast and you will help me.'

'But what about these hungry people?' Suraj asked.

'Feed them for now,' the rajah replied. 'In seven days' time, you will bring the bowl to me!'

And with that, the rajah mounted his horse and rode back to the palace. His chief advisor asked him about Suraj's gift, and the rajah explained what he had seen.

'Then we must take the bowl,' the chief advisor replied.

'Why?'

'Because no subject should have more power than the rajah,' the advisor said. 'Such treasure should not belong to a snivelling wretch who lives in a hut. It should be yours!'

The rajah's advisors sent out invitations across the land. A great feast was being prepared, and the richest people in the kingdom were invited. When the day came, Suraj trudged to the palace with his bowl. He was taken before the rajah, who asked how the bowl worked.

'You just ask for food,' said Suraj. 'It never fails.'

The rajah grinned and thought of the most delicious things he could imagine.

'Coconut pancakes and honey,' he began. 'Roasted lamb and spicy chicken, saffron rice and garlic naan! Pomegranates and mangoes, and juicy pineapples!'

Everything the rajah asked for appeared in an instant.

'Excellent!' said the rajah, before adding more to his feast.

Soon every table was overflowing with food and the rajah was ecstatic. His guests would be astonished and show him great respect.

The feast lasted for two days and was a huge success. The guests ate and drank until they were bursting, and then they ate some more. As they stuffed their faces, Suraj watched in sadness. Parvati's precious gift was being misused. And when the rajah decided to keep the magic bowl, Suraj was not surprised.

'But without it, I will starve,' he protested. 'As will many others . . .'

'Nonsense!' said the rajah. 'You'll be fine!'

Suraj shook his head in sorrow and went home.

For a whole year, Suraj survived on scraps, and by begging when he could. He grew bony and sick, and his life was full of misery. When Diwali was close, he went back to Parvati's temple, more desperate than ever. He arrived on the night before the festival to find the temple deserted. He wept in despair and offered prayer after prayer, but it was no use. Exhausted and starving, he collapsed and passed out.

Just as the first time, the goddess herself awoke him with a gentle nudge.

'Poor Suraj,' she said. 'What has happened to you?'

'Please, mighty Parvati,' he replied. 'I made a mistake and the bowl has been taken from me.'

Parvati's eyes began to glow with rage. 'WHO HAS DONE THIS?' she bellowed, frightening poor Suraj.

'The rajah,' Suraj sobbed, before explaining what had occurred.

Parvati listened in silence, and when Suraj was finished, she produced a wooden spoon from her robes.

'This rajah will pay for his heartless gluttony,' she said.

'How will he pay?' asked Suraj.

'From this moment the bowl will lose its magic!' said Parvati. 'Only you will be able to use it.'

She held out the spoon.

'Take this to the rajah,' she explained. 'Tell him that unless the bowl and spoon are used together, neither will work.'

'But he will just take the spoon too,' said Suraj.

'Oh, he might try,' said Parvati. 'But he will live to regret it! There's just one more thing to tell you . . .'

She whispered her last instructions to him, and then disappeared.

*

Suraj did as Parvati asked and soon found himself back before the irritated rajah.

'The bowl is broken!' the rajah explained. 'I have very important guests and can't feed them. Make it work!'

Suraj held up the spoon.

'You need to use this with it,' he said.

'The *spoon*?' asked a perplexed rajah.

Suraj nodded. The rajah took the spoon and asked the magic bowl for some food. Without warning, the wooden spoon jumped from the rajah's hands and started beating him.

'OW!!!!!!' the rajah wailed. 'Stop it, stop it!'

But the spoon continued to thrash him. The rajah's guards tried to catch it, but were too slow. The chief advisor tried and received a slap on the nose. No one could grab hold of it, and the rajah began to wail.

'Perhaps you should offer a prayer?' Suraj suggested. 'I always pray to the goddess Parvati . . .'

The rajah yelped again before doing what Suraj had said. Suddenly, a mighty gale roared through the palace and Parvati appeared on the rajah's throne. Everyone at court stood in shock and fear.

'STOP!' Parvati roared.

The spoon instantly fell to the floor and the rajah cried in relief.

'Oh, mighty Parvati,' said the rajah. 'I am grateful for your help.'

'BEAT HIM!' Parvati yelled.

The spoon shot up and began again.

'*No, not again!*' the rajah wailed. 'Please make it stop!'

Parvati stood and approached the beaten rajah.

'You will pay a heavy price for cheating Suraj,' she said. 'The magic bowl was my blessing to him. You have dishonoured me! And all for greed . . .'

'No, no!' the rajah begged. 'I would never disrespect you, mighty Parvati. Have mercy!'

Parvati thought for a moment and then took hold of the wooden spoon.

'Very well,' she replied. 'Your penance is simple. The bowl and the spoon will go with Suraj. You will also give him a splendid house and ten bags of gold . . .'

The rajah fell to his knees. 'Of course!' he replied. 'Anything . . .'

'That will be all,' said Parvati.

She gave Suraj the bowl and the spoon, and made to leave.

'And be warned,' she added. 'If you ever harm Suraj again, the spoon will find you, and it will bring more spoons with it.'

'Never!' said the rajah. 'The boy is free to go!'

Parvati turned to Suraj.

'Dear, kind Suraj,' she said. 'May you be blessed in this and many more lives. You are a fine young man.'

Then another gust of wind whistled through the palace, and Parvati was gone.

Suraj was given his house and money, but he never forgot his past. Each evening, he fed the poor and hungry, and each Diwali, Parvati returned to see him. He found a wife and had many children, and lived peacefully for the rest of his days.

The Peacock and the Crane

Ever since they were small, the peacock had teased the crane for being ugly. The peacock, with its blue and green feathers, which it spread into a wonderful fan behind its head, was mean and small-minded, and incredibly vain.

'Haha!' it would say, whenever it met the crane. 'Look at you – your feathers don't even match!'

And it was true. The crane's feathers were mismatched shades of brown and cream, and it had a white spot above its beady left eye. Its legs were long and spindly, and its feet too big. Whenever the crane saw its reflection in the nearby lake, it would begin to cry.

'Why am I so ugly?' it would wail. 'Oh why, oh why?'

And, urged on by the mean peacock, the other animals would join in and bully the crane without mercy.

'You look like you'll topple over!' the crocodile would snap.

'Your feet!' the tiger would roar. 'They're so big! How can you walk with feet so huge?'

'You're not even the same colour,' the monkeys would howl down from their branches. 'Poor, ugly crane – what use are you?'

The lonely and unhappy crane would bow its head, drink some water and then flap its wings as hard as it could. Flying high into the sky, it would try to forget the bullying, and enjoy its miserable life. But not even soaring on the warm currents of air soothed its sorrow.

'At least you can fly,' the toad had once said.

The toad was the crane's only friend. It too had been bullied since it was little. It was slimy and black, with warty skin and a bloated neck.

'So what if I can fly?' the crane had replied. 'They will still mock me for being ugly.'

The toad was wiser than the crane, and less bothered about its appearance.

'We are not put on earth to be pretty,' the toad replied. 'We are not being judged for our beauty. Toads look like toads and cranes look like cranes. That's just the way things are. Mother Nature made it so . . .'

'But why did Mother Nature give the peacock such fine feathers?' the crane asked.

The toad flicked out its tongue to catch a passing fly. As it chewed, it thought about how to reply.

'Look, dear crane,' the toad eventually said. 'Your feathers are ugly and the peacock's are beautiful, but so what?'

'It's not fair!' the crane replied.

'Forget about fair,' said the toad. 'What use are feathers if you can't use them to fly?'

'Huh?'

The toad gave a belch before continuing. 'The peacock's feathers may be glorious but it cannot fly. You, however, can go anywhere you please. I would love to have your powerful wings. One day, they might prove very useful indeed . . .'

'Thank you, brother toad,' said the crane, but it was not convinced. The ability to fly was fine, but it would still be ugly, no matter where it went.

'What an unfortunate life!' said the crane, hobbling away to jeers from the monkeys.

That summer, however, the crane would come to understand what the toad had meant. The season was longer than usual and much hotter. Each day the sun blazed down on the lake, making it drier and drier. The land was parched, the bushes and the trees were dry, and the animals began to suffer from their thirst. No one enjoyed that summer, and most had no idea what was just round the corner . . .

Across the lake, to the north, was a huge forest, and beyond that lay a small village. Most of the animals had never seen the village, except for the tigers, the monkeys and of course the crane. A boy called Gagan lived in the village, with his widowed mother and his three younger sisters. The drought had affected them too, and one evening, Gagan was ordered to fetch water by his mother.

'Bring as much as you can,' his mother told him. 'Your sisters need to drink something.'

So Gagan set off for the well, which was at the edge of the forest. The other villagers were desperate for water too, but most would not dare approach the well. Tigers had attacked three men as they drew water, and the whole village now lived in fear. Gagan, however, was determined to get water for his family.

'No tiger will attack me,' he said to himself. 'I am sure of it.'

And so he crept closer to the well, holding two wooden pails, and keeping a watchful eye on the trees. If he saw anything move, he would drop the buckets and draw the sharpened knife he'd hidden inside his shirt.

But soon, he couldn't even see the trees. Night had

drawn in quickly, and the shadows had grown long. Unable to see, he put down his buckets and found a match and candles in his pocket. He lit a candle and peered into the gloom.

Suddenly he saw something blink in the trees. It was the candle's flame, reflected in the eye of some creature. Since it was dark, and the other animals would be sleeping, Gagan realized that he was facing at least one tiger. And when the tiger gave a short growl, Gagan forgot his bravado. He panicked and dropped the candle, running for his life.

But the tiger did not follow him. The candle had fallen into a pile of dry sticks that caught fire instantly. Soon the flames grew fierce and touched the wooden pails that Gagan had left behind. The pails caught fire too, and then an abandoned plough, followed by the bushes and then the trees. As Gagan ran, and the tiger ran, they didn't realize something very important. The fire was out of control . . .

It blazed through the night, causing the villagers to abandon their village, and burned its way across the vast forest. And when morning came, the fire was still raging and had reached the lakeside. The crane, soaring above the flames and smoke that morning, spotted the danger at once and realized it had to warn the others.

It flapped its powerful wings and swooped round in a loop, heading to the far side of the lake. But the bushes and trees round its home were already ablaze, and it was too late to help.

The monkeys tried to hide in the trees but it was no use . . .

The tigers ran into the bush, but the flames followed even faster, and the tigers ran out of breath long before the fire . . .

The crocodile crawled back to the lake, but the water had long since dried up, and now it had nowhere left to hide from the thick smoke . . .

And the peacock, with its fine plumage, was trapped. Unable to fly, all it could do was strut around as the flames came closer.

The crane was desperate to save them all, even though they had been so cruel. But it could do nothing, as fire and thick smoke ruined the landscape. And then, in a stroke of great fortune, it spied its only friend. The toad was hopping this way and that, dodging the flames, crying out for help. The crane swept down, and as it came close, it opened its beak and grabbed hold of the toad. Together they soared up into the sky, leaving the devastation behind.

'Oh, wonderful crane!' the toad exclaimed. 'You have saved my life! You are a true friend!'

The crane could not speak with the toad in its beak, so it continued to fly away. It knew of a mighty river, running through the middle of an even greater forest, and decided to head there.

'You see?' the toad said as they flew. 'I told you that one day your powerful wings would turn into a blessing. What good are the peacock's glorious feathers now?'

And even though it knew the toad was right, and even though the peacock had bullied it, the crane was full of sorrow. It shed a tear for the peacock and all the other animals, and then flew on to their new home.

Punchkin

Many years ago there lived an unhappy rajah with seven beautiful daughters. Although the princesses were kind and lovely, the rajah's wife had died and he was lonely. He missed his wife terribly, and each day his youngest daughter, Balna, tried to cheer his spirits. But even though Balna was clever and funny and beautiful, the rajah remained full of sorrow, despite her efforts.

The rajah's subjects loved the princesses. They were kind and fair, and were often found serving the poor and needy. They also took turns to cook for their father, as he dealt with the affairs of his kingdom. When the prime minister, the prudhan, passed away in mysterious circumstances, the rajah grew even busier and rarely saw his daughters.

The late prudhan left a widow and one daughter. One evening, as Balna and her sisters prepared their father's meal, the widow appeared at the palace kitchen doors with her daughter, begging for a little food and a fire with which to cook it. The princesses welcomed them in. Soon the widow and daughter began to return each evening, and no one said anything about it.

Except for Balna, that is. The youngest princess had heard rumours about the widow and grew suspicious. The woman was pretty and charming, but she asked too many questions about the rajah. Why was she so interested in him? Balna, who was quick-witted and bright, began to suspect the widow. One evening she confided in her sisters, but they shook their heads.

'Don't be so unkind, Balna,' they said. 'She means no harm.'

Balna, however, was certain that the widow was up to no good. 'Please listen to me,' she begged. 'Why doesn't she cook in her own kitchen? She was hungry and we gave her food, but she has her own house. If we don't send her away, we will regret it some day.'

Her sisters ignored her pleas, and the widow's daily visits to the palace kitchens continued.

Then, one evening, the rajah, tired after a long day, sat

down for his dinner. As soon as he ate, however, he grew shocked. There, in his curry, was a lump of mud. He pushed the plates away but refused to blame his daughters. Since his wife's death, they had prepared his food with great love. A little mistake was easy to forgive. But when his curry continued to be spoiled day after day, he realized something was wrong. His food was being ruined on purpose.

The rajah decided to investigate. He asked his guards to drill a spyhole between a storeroom and the kitchen. Then, having hidden in the store, he watched as his beloved daughters cooked. He saw them wash his rice with great care, before cooking it perfectly. The same was true of his curry. Not once did they ruin the food.

Once prepared, each dish was placed next to the hearth, ready to be eaten. And, as the rajah looked on in astonishment, the prudhan's widow crept into the kitchen. She edged slowly towards the pots, looking this way and that. Then, taking a stick, she began to flick mud into the carefully cooked dishes.

The angry rajah ordered his guards to seize the widow at once, and bring her before him. He was furious by now, but when the woman arrived, she begged for mercy. She charmed him with her looks and her words, and very quickly the rajah's anger disappeared. Instead, he began to feel sorry for her. She was just a poor and lonely widow, looking after her only child.

'But why did you put mud in my curry?' the rajah asked.

The widow gave a girlish smile. 'Because I wished to meet Your Majesty,' the woman told him. 'I knew you would find out and send for me. The people say that you are handsome, clever and kind. It is true . . .'

Bewitched and flattered, the rajah grinned. He asked the widow to stay for dinner, and they talked long into the night. The rajah forgot all of his sorrows and felt happy at last. Over time, the couple grew closer, until finally they were married. The new rani moved into the palace with her daughter.

The rani was delighted at her good fortune. Her husband had left her penniless but now she would no longer have to beg for food or worry about money. She made the palace her own, and her daughter became the favourite at court. The seven princesses were banished to the kitchens and became little more than servants. The rani was mean to them, and scolded them every day, but the princesses didn't complain. Instead they treated their stepmother and her daughter with kindness and love. And, all the while, their father kept quiet.

Yet, the princesses were still a problem. The rani wanted her own daughter to become the rajah's favourite. Instead of being grateful for their kindness, the rani became even meaner to the princesses. Each day, she gave them nothing but bread to eat, and just a swig of water to drink. The seven princesses soon grew hungry and downhearted, but they were too kind to tell their father. They did not want the rani to get into trouble.

Instead, each morning they visited the tomb of their dead mother, and prayed for some help. One day, whilst they were crying, they heard the ground crack open. A tree began to grow from nothing. One minute it was a twig, and the next it became a beautiful citrus tree, laden with ripe green pomeloes. As the others sat staring in disbelief, Balna eagerly snatched a fruit and tore into it. The bright pink insides were fresh and sweet, and full of juice. Her sisters quickly joined in, but each time they took a fruit, another appeared in its place.

'It's Mother,' Balna told her sisters. 'She heard our pleas and has given us this tree. We must not tell anyone – it's our secret.'

Each day afterwards the princesses returned and ate from the tree. They soon grew strong and healthy again, and could not believe their luck. However, the rani quickly noticed the change in them.

'How can it be?' she asked her daughter. 'I only allow them scraps of food yet they never grow hungry or thin.'

'Perhaps I should investigate,' her daughter replied.

'Yes, my girl,' the rani agreed. 'You must discover their secret.'

The next morning, as the sun rose steadily in the clear

azure sky and a soft breeze whispered through the trees, the rani's daughter followed the princesses to their mother's grave. Hiding behind another tomb, she watched as they gathered the delicious pomeloes. But she did not take care, and Balna soon spotted her.

'Sisters!' she cried. 'The rani's daughter is watching us. Quick – we must stop her!'

But Balna's sisters did not agree.

'She's not her mother,' they told their youngest sibling. 'She would never be so cruel. Let's give her some of our fruit.'

They called to the rani's daughter, and when she approached, she told them not to worry.

'You're so kind,' she said, taking some fruit. 'I won't tell a soul, I promise.'

However, as soon as she got home, she told her mother of the magical tree. The cruel rani grew furious, flinging her dishes against a wall. She stormed to her bedchamber and took to her bed. She lay there for two days, until the rajah began to worry. He hurried to find her.

'My dear wife,' he said. 'Whatever is the matter?'

'I have a terrible headache,' replied the rani. 'I fear that I will die.'

'What can I do to help?' the rajah asked, with concern etched across his face.

'Someone has cursed me with black magic,' the rani told him. 'There is only one cure for me, my love.'

She told him of the pomelo tree growing by his dead wife's grave.

'The tree is evil,' she said. 'Unless you destroy it, I cannot be saved. You must kill it and make a tea from its roots. If I drink that, I will live.'

The fearful rajah summoned his guards at once, and sent them to destroy the pomelo tree. When they returned, the palace servants made tea from its roots. The rajah hurried to his wife's room.

'Drink quickly,' he insisted. 'You cannot die!'

Within minutes, the rani made a miraculous recovery. She jumped up from her bed and threw her arms round her husband. 'Thank you, oh, thank you!' she cried. 'You have saved my life!'

The rajah sighed with relief and promised his wife that he would never let her suffer again.

When the princesses found out, they wept bitterly. Balna realized the truth, and wanted to chastise her sisters for trusting their stepsister. Only she was too kind to hurt them with her words. Instead, she sat alone and wondered what they would eat now. As her sisters cried, Balna noticed something strange. Their mother's tomb was encircled by a narrow channel. Suddenly, it began to fill with a creamy substance.

Astounded, Balna stood and drew near, reaching in to touch the dense liquid. Putting a finger to her lips, she smiled. The thick cream was sweet and spicy, and instantly filled her belly. Then it began to harden, forming into delicious cake.

'Sisters!' Balna cried. 'Come quickly. Mother has saved us once again!'

The princesses crowded round and gasped in awe. Then, quickly, they pulled fat chunks of cake away, scoffing them with glee. It tasted of brown sugar and cinnamon, and cardamoms and coconut.

'It is amazing!' Balna's sisters cried.

'Yes, it is!' said Balna. 'Only, we *must* keep our secret this time.'

But once again, the cruel rani noticed how healthy the princesses remained, despite the death of their magical tree.

'Curses!' she cried. 'What is saving them now?'

The rani's daughter was eager to please her mother. She returned to her spying, and soon discovered the princesses' new secret. The following day, she did not hide. When Balna saw her approaching, she grew angry.

'Go away!' cried Balna, trying to shield the cake. 'You have betrayed us already!'

'No, no!' the rani's daughter replied. 'I didn't say anything! A guard saw you eating from the tree and told my mother.'

'Why should we believe you?' asked Balna.

'Because it's *true*,' her stepsister insisted. 'She doesn't even know I'm here! If she did, she'd beat me.'

Balna was about to reply when her sisters stopped her.

'Balna!' they said. 'Look how scared she is! She is trembling with fear. We must believe her!'

Ignoring Balna's suspicions, they revealed the secret of the cake and gave some to the rani's daughter. And once again, upon leaving them, the rani's daughter ran home to tell her mother.

The rani was enraged. She summoned her servants and ordered them to tear down the tomb. Then, taking to her bed once more, she sent for the rajah.

'I am gravely ill, my love,' she croaked. 'I am under another spell. I will die within days unless you do as I ask.'

The rajah grew tearful. 'Tell me what to do!' he cried. 'I will not let you die.'

The rani slowly shook her head. 'Only one thing can save me,' she said. 'But you won't do it, my love.'

'Anything!' the rajah cried. 'I swear on my honour that I will do anything!'

The rani spoke in a whisper, through forced tears. 'To save my life, you must kill your daughters,' she said.

The rajah's mouth fell open in disbelief.

'Then you must take their blood and smear it on my forehead,' the rani added.

'No,' the rajah whispered. 'There must be something else . . .'

'I'm sorry, my love,' the rani replied. 'There is nothing else. If I am to live, your daughters must die . . .'

The rajah broke down and wept, and cursed the heavens. He had sworn to keep his word, and he could not break that promise. With a heavy heart, he agreed to save the rani.

'I wish it were different,' the rani said. 'I love those girls. I cannot bear this.'

The rajah steadied himself and went off to find his daughters. He discovered them crying at their mother's ruined grave. As soon as he saw their faces, he realized that he could not harm them. He remembered each as a newborn, and each first step. They were his only treasures. Saddened but determined, he hastily hatched a plan.

'We never spend time together any more,' he said to them. 'Come, let your father take you on an adventure tomorrow.'

'That would be delightful, Father,' Balna replied. 'But are you unwell?'

'No, no, sweet Balna,' the rajah replied. 'Why do you ask?'

'You're as white as coconut flesh,' said Balna. 'As though you've seen a ghost.'

The rajah looked at the ruined grave and shook his head.

'It is nothing,' he replied.

They left early the next morning, and rode into the jungle. By a small stream, they found a clearing, where they played games and chatted. At lunch, the rajah's most trusted servants prepared a fire. The rajah made sweet rice pudding for his daughters, which they ate with delight. As the day grew warmer, the princesses began to fall asleep. Once they slept, the rajah's servants readied to leave. The rajah gazed lovingly at his children, then whispered to them.

'My poor, beautiful daughters,' he said, his heart breaking. 'It is better that you are left alone than die. Please forgive me . . .'

On his way back, the rajah shot and killed a deer and captured its blood in a jar. Once home, he spread the blood across the rani's forehead. Believing that her husband had done as she had asked, the rani instantly improved. The sorrowful rajah lost all strength. Depressed and full of sadness, he retired to his own chambers and locked the doors. And, with the princesses gone, the rani finally settled into a life of luxury with her daughter at her side.

As soon as they awoke, the princesses realized their fate. The jungle was dense, the plants and trees thick, and the shadows they cast very sinister. The princesses grew frightened, all except for Balna, who decided to act. As her sisters shouted for help, she went to the stream. Her father had taught her many things since her childhood. One lesson had involved streams. They always led somewhere.

'Stop shouting,' she told her sisters. 'There is no one to hear you, apart from tigers and bears. We will follow the stream.'

When her sisters looked unsure, Balna sighed. 'The stream flows to the south,' she pointed out. 'It must emerge somewhere. And along the way, there will be people who use its water. If we follow it, we can find help.'

They set off at once, and followed the flow for hours. The journey was difficult because the undergrowth was dense, and they were covered in scratches from thorny bushes. But soon the stream met a wider river, and there, on the bank, they found a camp. Around it sat seven young men, who saw the princesses as they approached. The youngest man stood to greet them. 'I am Prince Mohan,' he said. 'And these are my brothers. You look lost and tired – please let us help you.'

'My,' Balna replied, smiling at Mohan. 'What good luck! We would be very grateful for your help.'

As Mohan's brothers gathered round, the princesses introduced themselves. The brothers poured fresh water for their guests and cut up ripe mangoes.

'We have a deer roasting,' Mohan said. 'Please share it with us.'

That evening, the group washed and ate and chatted. Balna took the lead, explaining her situation to Mohan, who was awed by her beauty.

'We could take you home,' said Mohan.

Balna shook her head, her heart heavy with sorrow. 'Our father abandoned us,' she said.

'But that's terrible,' Mohan replied. 'Why would he do such a thing?'

'I don't know,' said Balna. 'But I do know he loves us. So there must be a very serious reason.'

'So you are all alone?' asked Mohan.

'We are,' Balna replied. 'We must find a new life.'

'Then come with us,' said Mohan. 'Our father will welcome you with open arms!'

Balna and her sisters discussed Mohan's offer, and agreed to go with them. What other choice did they have? As the sun rose, the princes packed up their camp, and they set off. The princes walked, and the princesses took their horses, and along the way they grew to become friends. When, a week later, they reached the princes' kingdom, they were warmly welcomed.

Soon, the seven princes fell in love with the seven princesses, and they were betrothed. On their wedding day, the entire kingdom came to watch, and there was great joy. Balna gladly married the wise and handsome Mohan, and was at last content. She and her sisters were safe and happy, and they had a new home.

A year later, Balna gave birth to a son. Her sisters had no other children, so the boy became the favourite of everyone, and they loved him as their own. They lived without care, their lives full of comfort and joy. Then, one morning, Prince Mohan went hunting with his servants. Hours became days, and days turned into weeks, yet Mohan did not return. Balna grew sick with worry, and was comforted by her sisters.

Mohan's brothers decided to search for him. The six brothers saddled their horses, loaded provisions, and set out to find Mohan. But their search was in vain, and soon they were lost too. The seven princesses, the rajah and the entire kingdom fell into grief. They were certain that the princes had met a wicked fate.

As Balna bathed her son one evening, a stranger arrived at the palace gates. The man wore a long black cloak and had a matching wispy beard. He told the guards he was a fakir – a wandering monk. He asked to see the princesses. The rajah's guards turned him away, but the fakir would not move. A servant overheard his request, and spoke up for him.

'It is bad luck to ignore a holy man,' said the servant. 'Have we not suffered enough?'

The guards stepped aside, and the servant took the fakir to the kitchens, where he was fed.

'Thank you for your kindness,' the fakir said. 'Your kingdom is cursed. Let me give you a blessing.'

When the servant failed to understand, the fakir explained.

'My name is Punchkin,' he said. 'I know your princes

have disappeared. I have come to bless the princesses. Perhaps that will help them.'

The servant was too afraid to ask the rajah, so he found Balna instead. He explained what Punchkin had said, and asked for advice.

'What harm can he do?' said Balna. 'I am happy to meet this fakir.'

'As you wish, Your Majesty.'

The servant hurried back to the kitchens where he found Punchkin entertaining the staff with jokes.

'Please follow me,' the servant said.

When Punchkin arrived, he gasped in surprise. Balna was even more beautiful than he had imagined.

'You are truly radiant,' he said.

Balna, surprised by Punchkin's comment, grew suspicious.

'Why would a fakir speak this way?' she asked.

'I am merely telling the truth,' said Punchkin. 'I was told you were beautiful, but you are more than that.'

'Silence!' replied Balna. 'No holy man would say such things!'

'You are correct, fair princess,' said Punchkin. 'I am no monk. I am a powerful magician and my wealth is extraordinary. Come away to my palace, and I will make you my bride!'

Holding back her anger, Balna responded calmly.

'Good sir,' she said. 'You are welcome to our food and drink. But you are not welcome to me.'

'I meant no disrespect,' said Punchkin.

Balna shook her head.

'I don't care,' she told him. 'My husband is missing, feared dead, and I have a son to raise. I will never leave with you!'

'But fine princess . . .'

'Leave at once!' Balna ordered. 'Or I will summon the guards!'

A vicious sneer spread across Punchkin's face, his eyes widening in rage.

'Mind your tongue!' he roared. 'I am Punchkin and no one defies me!'

Before Balna could scream, Punchkin produced a wand from his robes. With a single swish, he turned Balna into a little black dog. And leaving the infant in his cot, Punchkin led Balna away. At the gates, the guards asked where the dog had come from, and Punchkin smiled.

'Why, the dog is a gift from Princess Balna,' he replied. 'She is very grateful for my blessing.'

And with that, he left the palace, never to return.

As the years passed, Balna's sisters raised her son as their own. They could not bring her back, or the missing princes, but they made sure the boy grew into a fine young man. The young prince was named Nanda, which meant joy. He was strong and brave, and resembled his mother, with big eyes and clear skin. His friends often teased him for being so pretty, but Nanda did not care. He simply wanted his parents back. His aunts had never explained where his parents had gone, and he was desperate to know. When Nanda turned fourteen, his grandfather died, and Balna's sisters decided to tell him the truth.

As soon as he heard the truth, Nanda grew determined to find his parents and his uncles. The princesses grew anxious and warned him not to leave.

'We cannot lose you too!' they cried. 'You are our last hope, Nanda!'

'Please don't worry,' the young prince replied. 'I will find them, and I will return. I promise!'

A day later, Nanda began his quest. For many months he searched fruitlessly, from jungles to deserts, and across mountains and valleys. Then, after many hundreds of miles and almost losing hope, he reached a very strange country. It was like nothing he'd ever seen. Everywhere he saw oddly shaped rocks and trees that seemed almost human. In the distance, through a vast forest, he saw a magnificent palace sitting upon a mountain. Intrigued, he decided to pay the palace a visit, weaving his way through the forest for many days.

When he got to the mountain, he climbed a narrow path until he reached the plateau on which the palace stood. He found many more stone pillars, rocks and trees, each one oddly shaped, and beyond those, a small city. On its outskirts stood a little house, outside which sat an old woman.

As soon as she saw him, the woman ran over, waving her arms.

'No!' she cried. 'You must stop at once!'

'But why?' he asked.

'This is a terrible and dangerous place! Why have you come?'

'I am a prince,' Nanda explained. 'I am searching for my parents and my uncles. My mother was tricked by a wicked magician.'

The woman slowly shook her head. 'Then,' she said, 'perhaps you have found the right place.'

Prince Nanda's hopes soared.

'A powerful and wicked magician rules this place. He is a vicious and deceitful man. You see these rocks and stones, and the strangely shaped trees?'

'I noticed them at once,' the prince replied.

'They were living beings until the magician cursed them,' she revealed.

'My father was lost,' said Nanda. 'His six brothers came to find him, and they never returned.'

The old woman sighed. 'I know their story,' she said softly. 'They came here and were turned to stone.'

Prince Nanda grew angry. 'Where is this magician?' he demanded. 'I will avenge my family!'

'No, no!' the woman cried. 'You cannot match Punchkin. He is too powerful. He has turned hundreds of people and animals to stone. Do not anger him.'

Nanda felt his heart thudding inside his chest.

'Did you call him Punchkin?' he asked excitedly.

'Yes, boy,' the woman replied. 'That is his name.'

'Tell me, did he bring anyone else here? A princess, perhaps?'

The woman nodded. 'He keeps a beautiful princess hostage – in his palace.'

'What is her name?' asked Nanda.

The woman shrugged. 'I don't know,' she replied. 'But when he brought her here, she was a little black –'

'DOG!' yelled the prince. 'That is my mother!'

When he saw the woman's confusion, Nanda took her hand and led her indoors. There he explained his story, and the woman listened in horror. When he finished, she hugged him and told him how sorry she was.

'Will you help me?' asked Nanda.

'Help you?' the woman replied. 'Your only chance is to run. Go now, before he discovers your presence.'

'I cannot leave,' Prince Nanda told her. 'I have searched far and wide for my family. I must save them!'

'But he will curse you too,' the woman warned.

'Please,' begged Nanda. 'You must help me.'

'Very well,' the woman replied. 'But if anyone sees you, they will tell Punchkin. All strangers must be captured and sent to the palace. If you stay here, I must disguise you.'

The prince, eager to find his mother, agreed. The woman found some saffron and green sari material, and wound that round the prince. Then she covered his head with more fabric.

'There,' she said. 'You are very pretty, for a boy.'

'I feel ridiculous!' said Nanda.

'Never mind,' said the woman. 'At least you are disguised. If someone asks, you are my niece.'

For three days, the prince waited, helping the woman with her chores. When he went out for walks, he spoke to the neighbours, but no one suspected him. Then on the fourth morning he was in the garden when a tall man in black robes happened by.

'Who are you, girl?' asked the man, smoothing his wispy black beard. 'I haven't seen you before.'

The prince put on a quiet, high-pitched voice. 'This is my aunt's house,' he said. 'I am visiting her.'

'You are very pretty,' said the man. 'I am Punchkin – ruler of this kingdom.'

Prince Nanda felt his legs begin to tremble and his heart beat faster. Here was the man who'd taken his family. When he failed to reply, Punchkin continued, 'Tell me, pretty girl – will you do something for me?'

'Yes,' said Nanda. 'Anything, Your Majesty . . .'

'A beautiful woman lives in my tower. I would like you

to take her some flowers for me. The last flower girl displeased me, so I . . . let her go.'

'I would be happy to take her place,' said Nanda, wondering what fate the poor flower girl had met.

'Tomorrow, then,' Punchkin replied. 'Come to the palace before midday.'

The prince nodded and turned away, so that Punchkin did not see his excitement. Once the magician had gone, he ran into the house.

'He was here!' the prince said. 'Punchkin was here!'

He told the woman what had happened, and how he would soon see his mother again.

'But how will your mother know you?' asked the woman. 'You can't risk being discovered.'

The prince reached into his tunic, producing a chain upon which was a tiny golden ring.

'My mother gave me this,' he said. 'She will know it.'

'It is too dangerous, boy,' she replied. 'Wait and you will find another way.'

'No!' Prince Nanda told her. 'I am grateful for your help, kind woman, but I must save my mother!'

The woman realized that Prince Nanda would not change his mind, so she gave him another warning.

'Remember,' she said, 'Punchkin is wily and mistrustful. Do not give him any reason to suspect you. Your mother will be well-guarded.'

Next morning, Prince Nanda arrived at the palace, to

be met by Punchkin. In the magician's hands was a bunch of roses. 'Take these flowers and climb the tower,' Punchkin told him. 'And please be sure to return and tell me everything my princess says.'

'Of course, Your Majesty.'

Punchkin took a gold coin from his pocket. 'And this is your payment,' he said.

Prince Nanda took the money and the flowers, and entered the dark stairwell. The tower was tall and the steps narrow and worn. He wound his way to the top, where a guard sat by the only door.

'I bring flowers for the princess,' said Nanda.

The guard grunted before unlocking the door. Inside, Nanda found an apartment filled with luxurious furniture and fabrics, and the biggest bed he'd ever seen. But the room was gloomy and dusty, and seemed cold too. By the tiny window, he saw the woman he believed to be his mother. She was more beautiful than he'd ever imagined. Her hair was long and shiny, her eyes wide and deep brown, and her skin was like caramel. She eyed him without a word and nodded at a pile of dead flowers by the table.

'Leave them here!' the guard ordered.

Nanda fought the urge to call out to the princess, but he kept his nerve. Placing the flowers in a vase, he turned and left.

For three more days, Nanda took flowers to his mother,

but not once was he left alone. He grew frustrated and angry, and on the fourth evening, he decided to try a new plan.

'Are there tigers in the forest below the mountain?' he asked the old woman.

'Why, yes,' she replied. 'You must have seen them on your journey here?'

Prince Nanda shook his head. 'No, only jackals and bears,' he said.

'Why do you ask about tigers?'

Prince Nanda lowered his voice. 'I have an idea,' he told her. 'But I need your help . . .'

The next day, as Prince Nanda climbed the tower, a commotion began outside. Someone had spotted a tiger, loose in the streets. Punchkin's men ran to find the beast, before it attacked someone. When Nanda reached the door, the guard seemed confused.

'You must hurry!' Nanda told him. 'There is a tiger in the city!'

'But what about the princess?' the guard asked.

'I will wait here,' said Nanda. 'I'll give the princess her flowers and keep watch until you return. Hurry – I've heard terrible stories about Punchkin. Don't upset him . . .'

The guard shuddered at the thought of an angry Punchkin. Convinced that the girl was no threat, he unlocked the door and then ran downstairs. Nanda waited a while, and then entered the room. The princess sat at the window, her back to him, so he set down the white roses.

'Princess,' he said, still disguising his voice.

'Go away,' the princess replied.

'But, my lady . . .'

When the princess didn't respond, Nanda dropped his pretence.

'*Mother!*' he said in his own voice.

The princess turned and shot him a suspicious glare. 'Who *are* you?' she asked, peering through the gloom.

Nanda produced the ring from his clothes and stepped forward.

'You gave me this when I was born,' he explained. 'I am your son . . .'

Balna took a moment to register. Her eyes grew wide. She threw a hand over her mouth, to stifle her scream.

'Mother,' Nanda whispered through tears. 'I have found you . . .'

They held each other for a long while, crying all the while. When at last they let go, Balna grew frightened.

'Please,' she said. 'You must leave at once! If Punchkin discovers you, he will turn you to stone!'

But the prince stood fast. 'I have a plan, Mother, but I will need your help.'

'Anything,' said Balna. 'But hurry up. The guard will return soon.'

The prince smiled.

'Punchkin must have a weakness,' he said. 'If I am to rescue you, I must know what it is.'

'But how can I help?' asked Balna.

'I need you to find out,' Nanda told her. 'Perhaps you can make Punchkin trust you?'

Balna nodded.

'He has imprisoned me until I marry him,' she said. 'Perhaps if I agree, he will tell me everything.'

'It is our only hope,' Nanda told her. 'I'm sorry, but there is no other way.'

'I understand,' Balna replied. 'Now, go! The guard is coming back.'

'I shall return each day with flowers,' said Nanda. 'Do not fear, Mother. I *will* save you . . .'

The guard burst through the door, his face red.

'Did you find the tiger?' Nanda asked in his false voice.

'It was nothing,' the guard replied. 'Just some crazy old woman, seeing things.'

As Nanda descended, his heart felt light and he grinned.

A week later, Punchkin visited Balna. She smiled when he entered and asked him to sit.

'I realize my mistake,' she told him. 'And I wish to leave this tower.'

'Yes, the flower girl told me,' said Punchkin. 'Does that mean you will marry me?'

'Perhaps,' Balna replied.

'Then we shall wait no longer!' the excited magician cried.

'No, no,' said Balna. 'You must give me time. We should have dinner and talk. Get to know each other . . .'

'Hmmm,' said Punchkin. 'Perhaps you are right. After all, you have been imprisoned for a long time.'

'Yes,' Balna agreed. 'We have been enemies for too long. We should be friends before we marry.'

'Then come with me!' Punchkin declared. 'You will live in the palace, with servants to attend to your every need.'

'I would like the flower girl to be my maid,' said Balna. 'She is lovely and loyal . . .'

'Of course,' smiled Punchkin. 'Anything you desire, my princess . . .'

Balna's new quarters were luxurious, and she was very comfortable, but she was also worried. What if Punchkin didn't tell her his secrets? What if he found out she was playing a trick? The magician visited every evening, and Balna did her best to gain his trust. But after five days, she still wouldn't commit to a wedding and Punchkin grew impatient.

'I am no fool,' he told her on the sixth night. 'Your beauty is great but I cannot be tricked! You will accept marriage by morning, or you will return to the tower!'

Balna grew frightened and thought quickly.

'There is one thing more,' she said. 'If I am to marry you, I must know if you are truly invincible.'

Punchkin seemed puzzled.

'Why ask this?' he replied.

'Because you must have made many enemies,' said Balna. 'I have already lost a father, a husband and a son. If I marry you, how do I know you won't be taken too?'

Punchkin nodded. 'Because I am not like other men,' he told her. 'They are weak and I am strong.'

'Surely any man can be killed?' said Balna, pretending to be sad at the idea.

'Not I,' Punchkin boasted. 'The source of my powers is well hidden.'

'But nothing cannot be found,' said Balna, hoping he'd explain further.

'Haha!' said Punchkin. 'My power resides in a faraway land, through deserts and jungles. There is a clearing there, and within lies a circle of palm trees. I have placed six clay water pots there, one on top of the other. The bottom vessel is empty save for a small cage. And inside that cage lives a green parrot . . .'

'A parrot?'

'Yes . . .' Punchkin replied, smoothing his beard. 'I cannot be killed unless it dies first . . .'

'But what if . . . ?'

'No one will ever find it!' Punchkin declared. 'And even

if they do, a thousand genies guard it. They would kill anyone who approached.'

Balna nodded.

'So you must not worry,' added Punchkin. 'I will never be killed.'

'Very well,' said Balna. 'Give me another month, kind sir. And I promise, I shall marry you then. You have my word.'

Punchkin, despite his impatience, grew excited and agreed at once. He rushed off to plan the momentous day.

When Prince Nanda returned as the flower girl, Balna told him everything, and begged that he leave at once.

'Go now, my son,' she wept, 'live your life. I will stay and bear my burden. I am simply happy to see your face one last time.'

'No, Mother,' Nanda replied. 'I will find Punchkin's parrot and set you free. Keep him busy until I return.'

'But what will I say about the flower girl?' asked Balna.

'Tell him that I've returned to my parents,' said Nanda. 'Be strong, my mother. Fortune is on my side. I will not fail you.'

Prince Nanda left that evening, packing a few belongings and some food and water. Stealing one of Punchkin's horses, he descended the mountain path and rode into the great forest. With no idea where he was going, he travelled for many days, until the forest became a thick jungle. That night, he sat down under a tall papaya tree and slept. Soon, a soft rustling and hissing awakened him. He sat up quickly, and saw a giant serpent. It slithered towards an eagle's nest in the branches above, where two eaglets sat. Nanda jumped to his feet, drew his sword and killed the snake with a single stroke.

Up above, he heard eagles cry, their mighty golden wings flapping. The eaglets' parents had returned. Spotting the dead snake, and the prince with his sword drawn, they landed at his feet. They were almost as tall as Nanda, and magnificent to behold.

'Thank you, oh, thank you!' the mother eagle cried out. 'You have saved my children!'

'I could not let it eat them,' the prince replied.

'That serpent has plagued every bird in the jungle,' said the father eagle. 'And now it is dead. You have blessed us, stranger.'

'My name is Nanda,' said the prince. 'And now we are friends.'

The prince sat down as the mother eagle took food to her young. Then she flew off to find fruits for the prince to eat.

'Where are you from, Nanda?' the father eagle asked.

'A place far away,' said Nanda. 'I am a prince and I am trying to save my mother.'

Slowly he told his tale, as the father eagle listened. The mother soon returned with mangoes for the prince, which he ate whilst talking. Eventually he described Punchkin's evil deeds and the location of his parrot.

'We know it!' the eagles replied in unison.

'The exact place?' asked Nanda, jumping to his feet in urgency.

'Yes,' said the father eagle. 'It is very far away, but I will take you there.'

'You are very kind,' said Prince Nanda, 'but I cannot take you away from your young.'

'Now that the serpent is dead,' said the father eagle, 'there is nothing to fear. Besides, I am forever in your debt.'

Time was against him, and Prince Nanda realized that he needed the eagle's help.

'Very well,' he said.

With no time to lose, the father eagle spread his enormous wings and Nanda climbed on to his back. Away they flew, higher and higher, until they reached the clouds. They flew tirelessly for three days, until finally they reached Punchkin's secret place. When the prince saw the circle of palm trees, he wept with joy.

It was noon, and the heat was intense. Each of the one thousand genies had fallen asleep. All around them, the prince saw the spoils of a great feast. Yet they could not land, in case they disturbed the evil spirits.

'I shall fly down with you,' said the eagle. 'If I knock over the water pots, you can grab the parrot.'

'We must be quick,' said Prince Nanda. 'The genies will wake up, and we cannot let them catch us.'

The father eagle nodded. 'Don't worry,' he said. 'I am too fast for them. Ready . . .?'

'Yes,' said Nanda, holding tight.

Down they swooped, as the air rushed past. They swept into the clearing and the eagle used its legs to topple the water pots. One by one, the pots crashed and shattered, until the last one fell open. The green parrot squawked in delight, and tried to take flight. But Nanda was too quick. He snatched the parrot with one hand, and rolled it up into his cloak. The evil genies woke and howled with rage, but far too late.

Before they could move, the eagle was soaring back into the clouds at dazzling speed. This time Nanda shrieked with delight, knowing that his mother would soon be saved. And when eventually they arrived back at the nest, the prince fell to his knees and thanked the eagles.

'Stay a while,' said the mother eagle. 'Stay and take supper with us.'

'You are very kind,' replied the prince, 'but I must leave at once. There is no time to lose!'

The father eagle spread his great wings once again. 'Then let me take you,' he said.

'But you have done so much for me,' said Nanda. 'I cannot put you in danger too.'

'You saved two children,' said the father eagle. 'This will be my second thank you.'

'Very well,' said Nanda. 'But after this, your debt to me is paid.'

Fearing that Punchkin might harm his new friend, the prince asked to be taken to the foot of the mountain. The eagle agreed, and they left that evening. By sunrise three days later, the prince had returned to Punchkin's kingdom.

Saying goodbye to the eagle, he ascended the mountain path, ready to face his enemy. And when he reached the house of the woman who had helped him, she held him tight.

'Dear boy!' she said. 'You have come to save us all!'

'Yes,' the prince replied. 'And there is not a moment to lose!'

He hurried to the palace, and at the gates, he took the parrot from its hiding place. Punchkin was in his courtyard, and sensed the parrot's presence immediately. He rushed to the gates, and froze in terror when he saw Nanda.

'Boy!' he demanded with a shaky voice. 'Where did you get that parrot? Give it to me at once!'

'No, no,' said Prince Nanda. 'This parrot is a dear friend.'

'Dear boy,' said Punchkin, 'I pray thee – the parrot, please . . .'

The magician held out a quivering hand. As he trembled

and shook, his servants began to gather, whispering amongst themselves.

'I said no,' the prince replied.

Punchkin thought quickly, his hands shaking in fear. 'Sell it to me, then,' he said. 'I will pay anything you ask!'

'Sir,' replied the prince, 'I will not sell my parrot.'

Punchkin's anxiety grew.

'Please, young man!' he cried. 'I will give you anything. *Anything*, I say!'

'Then set the seven brothers you turned into rocks free at once!' the prince demanded.

With a swish of his wand, Punchkin did as the prince asked.

'There,' he said. 'Now give me my parrot!'

The prince ruffled the bird's green feathers.

'Not yet!' he replied. 'Free every soul that you have ever cursed . . .'

Punchkin waved the wand yet again, and across his kingdom, the accursed were set free.

'It is done!' he cried. 'My parrot!'

The palace gardens burst into life. All around, rocks and trees and stones and shrubs became kings and princes, queens and princesses. Mighty horse-mounted warriors broke free of their torment, alongside many hundreds of servants and pages and attendants.

'My parrot!' Punchkin bellowed. 'Give me my –'

The prince took the parrot by its neck and tore off its left wing. As he did so, Punchkin's left arm fell off.

'Please . . .!' shrieked Punchkin.

The prince tore off the parrot's right wing and Punchkin's right arm fell away too.

'*ARRRGGGHHHHH!*' squealed the magician, falling to his knees.

The prince tore away the parrot's left leg, and Punchkin's left leg followed.

'*Noooo!!!!!!!!*'

The prince removed the parrot's right leg and Punchkin's right leg soon followed.

'*MERCY . . . !!!*' screamed Punchkin. 'I beg you, young sir!'

Nothing remained, except for Punchkin's limbless torso. Yet still the wicked magician begged and pleaded, and offered limitless wealth.

'Just give me my parrot,' he whispered.

The prince nodded. 'Here,' he replied. 'Take your parrot.'

He wrung the parrot's neck, and threw it at the magician. Punchkin's head twisted with a sickening wrench and he screeched in agony, Then, with a terrible groan, Punchkin fell dead at last.

That evening, the people of many, many kingdoms rejoiced at Punchkin's demise. His palaces and all of his wealth were shared amongst his long-suffering people. And the young prince was reunited with his mother, his father and all six of his uncles. After saying a tearful goodbye to the old woman, Prince Nanda led his family on their long journey home.

The Sun and the Moon

Jeet Singh watched his father tether the water buffalo and trudge wearily into the house. After a hard day of farming, Jeet's father was tired and hungry. He washed his hands and face, and then sat with a glass of milk.

'Father,' said Jeet. 'Will you tell me a story?'

'Of course, my son,' his father replied.

The previous evening had seen a full moon, something Jeet had always found fascinating. He wondered where the moon had come from, and the sun too.

'Tell me about the sun and the moon,' Jeet said.

'What about them?' his father asked.

'Where did they come from?' said Jeet, sitting down next to his father.

'Oh,' said his father, 'there are many stories. My favourite is about sweets.'

'Sweets . . .?'

Jeet grew excited at the thought of sweets and his father smiled.

'Are you ready?'

Jeet nodded.

'Once,' said his father, 'there lived a brother and sister . . .'

The boy was called Sun, and the girl was named Moon. Their mother was a widow, and her life was hard. One day, Sun and Moon were invited to a party. Their mother couldn't go with them, so she washed and dressed them, and sent them on their way.

'Bring back some sweets for me,' she said.

Sun and Moon had a wonderful time. The party was exciting and fun, and there were mountains of delicious food. When the time came to leave, their host gave Sun and Moon a big bag of sweets each.

'Thank you,' said Moon, because she was always polite.

But her brother, Sun, wasn't as well behaved. Sun was moody and naughty, and very, very greedy. Instead of thanking their host, he opened his bag, took a sweet and ate it.

They walked home, and on the way, Moon was happy.

She loved her mother dearly, and couldn't wait to give her some sweets.

'But then you won't get any,' said her brother.

'Oh, Sun,' said Moon. 'I ate so much at the party. I don't *need* any more sweets.'

Sun shook his head in disbelief. 'But they're delicious!' he said. 'I'm going to eat all of mine.'

And he did. By the time they reached their house, Sun's bag was empty. Their mother was very pleased to see them, and made a fuss.

'My beautiful, wonderful children,' she said. 'Did you have fun?'

'Yes, Mother,' said Moon. 'It was lovely. I got a bag of sweets but I want you to have them.'

'Thank you, Moon,' said their mother. 'You are always so generous.'

Sun didn't say a thing. That night, as his mother and sister slept, he crept through the house. He found the bag of sweets on the table and smiled. One by one, he ate them all, until his belly ached and his tongue grew furry with sugar. Then he crept back to bed and fell fast asleep.

In the morning, his mother was furious. 'What happened to my sweets?' she asked.

'I don't know,' said Moon. 'Where did they go?'

Sun shrugged. 'Maybe a mouse ate them?' he said.

'A mouse?' said their mother. 'Do you think I'm a fool? I know you ate them!'

Sun tried and tried to convince her, but his mother would not listen. Instead, she made a sorrowful prediction.

'Sun,' she said. 'You are rude and misbehaved, and you tell so many lies. If you're not careful, you will end up burning with envy and greed.'

Sun sneered. 'At least I won't be timid and boring like her!' he shouted, pointing at his sister.

'Ah,' said their mother. 'You're very wrong. Moon is kind and generous. She will become a calming light in people's lives. She will radiate with goodness and joy forever . . .'

And so it proved.

Jeet's mother heard her husband's story and frowned.

'No, no,' she said, pulling Jeet to her. 'That's not the story, my son.'

'But Father said . . .'

Jeet's mother shushed him and smiled.

'Your father doesn't know the *real* story,' she teased. 'Sun and Moon *were* brother and sister, but there weren't any sweets . . .'

'No sweets?'

'No,' said Jeet's mother. 'Now, let me tell you what really happened . . .'

Sun and Moon lived a hard life in a small hut. Their mother had raised them alone, and was often very tired. On one such day, she asked her children to do her chores.

'Moon,' she said. 'There is no bread for supper. I would like you to make the dough and knead it. And when it is ready, you must make our food for us.'

'Yes, Mother,' replied Moon. 'You just take a rest.'

Moon was a calm and well-behaved daughter. Her kindness had no end, and she was always full of joy.

'Sun?' said their mother.

'I'm busy!' Sun replied.

'Listen to me,' said their mother. 'Without a fire, Moon cannot bake our bread. I would like you to collect kindling and light a fire for your sister.'

'Why can't *she* do it?' asked Sun. 'I can't do *everything* . . .'

'You must share the chores,' said their mother. 'Light the fire, but be careful to watch over it. Otherwise it might grow too big.'

Sun huffed and stormed outside to find kindling. Unlike his sister, Sun was rude and naughty. He hated being told what to do, and never shared anything. Even so, he did as he was told, and soon the hearth danced with flames.

'There,' he said to Moon, as their mother slept on her string bed.

'Thank you, brother,' said Moon. 'Now, if you could just help me to shape the dough, I can . . .'

'What?' snapped Sun. 'Why should I help you? I've done my job . . .'

And out he went again, forgetting all about his mother's

warning. Moon soon needed more water, but found the buckets empty. Fetching water was one of Sun's tasks, but he hadn't done it. Shrugging off his failure, Moon grabbed a bucket and went to the nearest well. Inside, however, the fire began to grow and grow. A tiny glowing ember popped and landed on a piece of muslin, setting it alight. Their mother, her nose tickling, opened her eyes and saw the flames. She screamed and ran for the door, as the fire began to blacken the ceiling.

Outside, she saw the empty water buckets and grew angry. With nothing to douse the flames, the hut was soon ablaze. As Sun and Moon came running, their mother was furious.

'SUN!' she yelled. 'Look what your selfishness has done!'

'But, Mother, I . . .'

'ENOUGH!' their mother yelled. 'We have lost everything.'

And then she sat and wept. And through her tears, she made a prediction.

'Moon,' she whispered. 'You will always be peaceful and give people solace, but your brother will not be so fortunate . . .'

She looked up at her lazy and selfish boy, and shook her head in grief.

'Sun,' she said. 'As this fire burns, so will you – relentless and unforgiving, for eternity . . .'

*

Jeet looked at his parents.

'I'm confused,' he said. 'Which story is true . . .?'

'They're just myths,' said his father.

'But I still don't know where the Sun and Moon came from,' said Jeet.

'Never mind,' said his mother. 'I'm sure you'll find out one day. Now it's time for supper . . .'

The Tiger, the Brahmin
and the Jackal

One day, a huge tiger was strolling through a forest when it fell into a hunter's trap. Caged and angry, the tiger roared so loudly that every animal nearby ran away. It tried in vain to escape, rolling and snarling and biting, but the cage held fast. Eventually the tiger grew tired and gave up, slumping on its huge orange paws.

It grew hungry and afraid, but soon a kindly Brahmin happened upon the trap. The tiger sat up at once and called out.

'Oh, holy man!' it cried. 'Release me from this cage, I beg you!'

'I won't, friend,' the Brahmin replied. 'Although I cannot stand to see a fellow creature suffer, I am afraid of you. If I release you, you might eat me.'

'No, no!' the tiger declared. 'Why would I eat you for showing kindness? I promise on my children's lives, I will not attack you. If you save me, I will serve you.'

The tiger began to sob and wail, and plead with the holy man. Soon the Brahmin found his heart melting, and he stopped being afraid. How could he let this magnificent animal die?

'Very well,' the Brahmin agreed. 'But you must promise not to devour me.'

'I promise, I promise,' the tiger replied. 'I will be in your debt forever.'

The Brahmin edged closer to the cage, and untying the thick ropes, set the beast free. The tiger jumped from its prison, snarling and snapping.

'You foolish man!' it roared. 'I have been trapped for many days and my belly aches with hunger! Why should I not eat you?'

The Brahmin, realizing his mistake, began to tremble. He fell to his knees and begged for mercy.

'But I saved you from certain death!' the priest cried. 'How can you betray such kindness?'

'I am only doing what a tiger must do,' the great beast replied.

'But what about your karma?' the Brahmin asked. 'If you are so wicked, you will be reborn as a lower being!'

The tiger thought for a moment, and then shook its mighty head. 'Karma does not bother me,' it said. 'But you were very kind. Perhaps I shall give you a chance . . .'

'Anything, kind sir!' the Brahmin pleaded.

The tiger considered this and then declared, 'You must find three things and ask their advice. Should I eat you, or let you go? Whatever they say, I will accept. But you cannot ask any humans . . .'

'Agreed!' said the Brahmin.

Firstly, the Brahmin approached a sacred fig tree – a peepal. It stood tall and stout, its branches rich with lush foliage and heavy with fruit.

'Dear blessed tree,' said the Brahmin. 'I saved this tiger from certain death and now it wishes to eat me. What do you think it should do?'

The tree considered the priest's words a moment before it replied.

'You cannot complain!' it said. 'I give shelter to all humans who pass under my branches, no matter who they are. Yet still they cut me down and feed my leaves to their cattle! They take my fruits without a care about me. Why should I care what this tiger does?'

'Yes, but . . .' began the Brahmin.

'Enough!' said the tree. 'Go now and meet your fate!'

As the sorrowful Brahmin trudged away, the tiger was amused.

'That is one vote for me,' it said. 'My stomach is already rumbling . . .'

Next, whilst passing a field, the Brahmin spotted a powerful water buffalo, yoked to a waterwheel that it turned very slowly. Confident that the buffalo would help him, the Brahmin felt a little better. As they approached the well, the water buffalo stopped and watched them.

'Oh, mighty and hardworking buffalo,' said the Brahmin. 'I am caught in a terrible dilemma. I was hoping you might help me?'

The Brahmin explained his troubles, as the tiger lapped cool water from a puddle by the well. But the water buffalo scoffed and nodded to its yoke.

'You cannot expect help from me!' it said. 'When I was young and still gave milk, the farmers fed me delicious foods. But when the milk ran dry, they left me here, to toil in the sun. I gave them everything and now they feed me rubbish!'

'A terrible thing, I agree,' said the Brahmin, 'but . . .'

'Go now, wretch!' said the buffalo. 'I don't care about your problems!'

The Brahmin, now certain that the tiger would devour him, turned away.

'I think you will taste better with a little salt and pepper,' the tiger teased. 'But, first, let us find number three.'

The Brahmin refused to go on. Looking down, he saw the dirt path on which they stood. He decided to ask the dry earth what it thought, sure that the tiger would eat him regardless. The tiger smiled as it waited for a reply.

'You poor priest,' said the path. 'You were wrong to trust this beast. People use me every day, rich and poor, yet what do I get in return? My surface is scarred with potholes and cracks, and parched of water. I am only here to bear the weight of others. No one cares about me, do they?'

The Brahmin sat down in utter despair.

'So why should I care for you?' the path added.

'Eat me now!' the Brahmin wailed. 'I have nothing else to ask!'

However, the tiger shook its head. 'We must return to the forest,' it said. 'If I eat you here, other humans will see and they will kill me. I need privacy.'

So back to the forest the poor Brahmin trudged, trailing in the tiger's wake. And just as they reached the clearing where the tiger had been caged, they crossed the path of a jackal with mottled brown and white fur. The jackal smiled warmly as they approached.

'My dear priest!' it said. 'You look so gloomy. Whatever is the matter?'

The Brahmin explained his wretched story, before the tiger stepped forward.

'Be gone, jackal!' it roared. 'This man is my feast, not yours!'

'But,' the jackal replied, 'I am very confused. How did this man set you free?'

Once again, the Brahmin explained what had happened.

'I'm terribly sorry,' the jackal said. 'I seem to be going deaf. Did you say *cage*?'

'YES!' roared the tiger.

'May I *see* this cage?' the jackal replied. 'Just before you eat him? I do not wish to be trapped too, brother tiger.'

The tiger agreed and took the jackal to its former prison.

'So, let me see,' said the jackal. 'The *priest* was in the cage and you, brother tiger, happened to walk by . . .?'

'No, you idiotic, insignificant thing!' the tiger growled. '*I* was in the cage and the priest walked by!'

'I see,' the jackal said. 'So I was in the cage . . . no, wait. Oh dear, I am so terribly confused! I fear I shall *never* understand because I am so silly. You enjoy your dinner, brother tiger . . .'

'You *will* understand!' the tiger insisted. 'I'll *make* you understand!'

'But I'm so foolish,' said the jackal. 'Are you *wise* enough to show me?'

The tiger resisted the temptation to gulp down the idiotic jackal. Instead, he spoke slowly, so that it might finally comprehend.

'Look,' the tiger said. 'I am a *tiger* and *I* was in the cage . . .'

'Yes, brother.'

'And *he* is the Brahmin.'

'Yes, brother, do continue . . .'

The tiger nodded towards the trap.

'And *that* is the *cage*, you see . . .?'

'Yes . . . er . . . no, actually, I don't.'

'*ARRRRGGHHHHHHH*!' the frustrated tiger bellowed.

'A moment,' said the jackal. 'I understand all of that. But how did you get *into* the cage . . .'

'The *usual* way!' the tiger replied. 'How else?'

'But what *is* the usual way, brother?' the jackal asked. 'I cannot see how . . .'

The tiger, its patience finally gone, exploded in fury. 'Like *this*, you utterly ridiculous animal!'

And into the cage it jumped.

'Oh,' said the jackal. '*Now* I understand . . .'

Quickly, the jackal slammed the cage door shut, holding it until the Brahmin managed to lock it again.

'Perfect,' the jackal said to the Brahmin. 'Now, gentle priest, maybe you should run home and ignore any trapped tigers that you come across?'

The Brahmin, without a single word of thanks, turned and fled for his life. The jackal sighed and walked on through the forest.

To Catch a Thief

One afternoon Birbal went strolling through the palace gardens. It was a glorious day, full of sunshine and the chatter of colourfully plumed birds. A gentle breeze cooled the skin and the aroma of spices hung lightly in the air. It was a day to be joyful, a day for celebration.

Yet on entering the walled courtyard of Akbar's palace, he discovered one of the emperor's ministers, Fazal, looking distraught.

'Whatever is the matter?' Birbal asked.

Fazal bowed his head. 'I have been robbed,' he replied. 'My apartments were ransacked and everything of value taken.'

Birbal was stunned. Who would do such a thing at the royal palace? It was unthinkable.

'Let us find the emperor at once,' Birbal told him. 'This cannot be allowed to happen!'

Akbar's astonishment mirrored that of his best friend and advisor, Birbal.

'Never!' he bellowed. 'We shall catch this thief at once!'

'There are no clues to his identity,' said Fazal. 'He left nothing behind to give himself away.'

Birbal nodded. 'If Your Majesty wishes,' he said, 'I can make enquiries.'

Akbar agreed. 'Dear Birbal,' he said, 'my honour and the honour of my court is at stake. I cannot have my subjects thinking my own palace complex is insecure. Please catch this man quickly.'

'I shall,' Birbal replied. 'But in order to catch a thief, I need to think as a thief . . .'

Akbar squinted. 'I do not understand.'

Birbal dismissed Fazal and leant close to his friend.

'Let me explain,' he whispered, mindful that his eternal foe, Abdul Qadir, and the other courtiers were close at hand. In order to succeed, Birbal needed utmost secrecy.

That night, as the moon loomed large and full in the heavens, and everyone else slept, Akbar and Birbal edged their way through the numerous palace buildings. Dressed from head to toe in black cotton, with more black fabric tied round their faces, they resembled thieves themselves.

'This is ridiculous!' Akbar whispered to Birbal. 'I have no need to sneak about. I am the emperor.'

'And as emperor, the guards would not question how you found yourself in any of the apartments,' Birbal explained. 'We need to work out how the thief managed to get past everyone twice. To do that, we must not be seen either.'

'*Twice?*' said Akbar. 'You mean this man has struck before?'

Birbal shook his head, pulling Akbar into the shadows just as two guards walked by.

'No,' said Birbal. 'I mean he got in *and* out, without being seen . . . The palace complex is vast and heavily guarded, so how did he manage such a feat?'

Akbar nodded, and not for the first time, felt slightly dim in Birbal's presence. The palace complex *was* secure, as Birbal had said. There were men at each outer entrance, more men at the door to each building, and yet more who made regular patrols on foot.

'You are far wiser than me, Birbal,' said Akbar. 'I am glad that we are friends and not enemies.'

They waited until the patrol had moved on before creeping towards Fazal's apartment. On the way, they passed the women's quarters and several other rooms used by Akbar's attendants.

'This scoundrel could have seen the women asleep!' said Akbar. 'This is terrible!'

'Fear not, my friend,' said Birbal. 'We shall have him.'

At Fazal's door, Birbal tried the handle. The door, as was the usual practice, had been locked from within. No outsider would have access to the keys. Even the duplicates were kept in the treasury building.

'See if you can find an object with which to unlock the door,' Birbal said.

Yet they found nothing. If the thief had entered this way, either he had keys or else had broken the lock. Birbal was already aware it could not have been the latter. The door was not damaged in any way, and Fazal had not reported anything similar.

'Perhaps he came in through the windows?' Akbar suggested.

'Let us see,' Birbal replied.

Once again, they crept back along dark, deserted corridors, dodging past any moonlit windows quickly. Several times they hid in alcoves and shadows, as patrols went by. The only sounds came from outside – the chirping of crickets and the fluttering of giant moths, the hooting of owls, and the distant howling of wolves from deep within the forests. Occasionally green and yellow lizards, no longer than a man's hand, emerged from their hides to observe Birbal and Akbar's mission.

'Impossible!' Akbar said, as they entered the walled

courtyard that lay below Fazal's apartments. 'No thief could have managed this!'

Birbal ignored him. Instead he counted openings in the wall, on the same floor as Fazal's rooms. At six, he was sure he stood directly below Fazal's windows.

'Can you see a ladder or anything else the thief might have climbed?' asked Akbar.

'No,' Birbal replied. 'There is nothing.'

Underneath the window, the moon lit the wall brightly. It showed no scratches in the stone where a ladder might have rested. The flagstones were similarly untouched.

'There is nothing to suggest he entered this way either,' said Birbal. 'And the window is far too high for him to have jumped up.'

'Then I fear all is lost,' Akbar replied. 'I shall, of course, recompense Fazal for his woes, but . . .'

'Your Majesty,' Birbal said, 'this means nothing.'

'Nothing?'

Birbal nodded. 'We have simply disproved the notion that our thief was a stranger.'

Akbar thought for a moment.

'So if he didn't come from outside the palace . . .' Birbal added, nudging Akbar's thoughts along.

'He must have come from within!' said Akbar excitedly.

'Our thief is one of us,' Birbal confirmed.

The following morning, having barely slept for concern, Akbar ordered every person within the palace complex to the great banqueting hall. Despite its vast interior, even this room could not hold everyone, and many worried subjects stood quietly outside. Inside, Akbar made a declaration. 'My trusted friend, Birbal, wishes each of you to take part in a test,' he said. 'No person shall refuse, no matter what their reason. Is that understood?'

Inside and out, everyone nodded in consent. The emperor's advisors stood together but only Abdul Qadir spoke up.

'What can we do to help, Majesty?' he asked, hopeful of gaining much-needed favour, and desperate to outshine Birbal, whom he despised.

'Birbal will handle everything,' Akbar told him. 'Please listen to his every command.'

A moment later, Birbal appeared, leading a donkey. Akbar's subjects murmured and whispered, each one confused. Akbar forced himself not to smile. Birbal tied the donkey to a stone pillar, securing its legs so that it could not kick out. Round the donkey, several guards erected a flimsy, wood-framed tent. Once the donkey was out of sight, Birbal spoke to the waiting subjects.

'Each person must go into the tent, lift up the donkey's tail, and say these words. *I HAVE NOT STOLEN*. There must be absolutely no exceptions. Is that clear?'

Once again, everyone nodded, despite a growing sense of nervous bemusement amongst the crowd. Birbal took a seat next to Akbar and waited. Slowly, and one by one, each person entered the tent, before retaking their positions. The entire process took a great deal of time, and Akbar amused himself by taking lunch and, afterwards, asking Birbal to set him riddles. The final one had Akbar mightily perplexed.

'What tastes better than it smells . . .?' he asked for the fourth time. 'The answer could be many things!'

'There is just one answer, my friend,' said Birbal, yawning. 'This is taking far too long . . .'

'A *tongue*!' Akbar finally yelled. 'It's a tongue!'

Birbal nodded, as a guard approached them.

'We are finished, Your Majesty,' the guard said.

'At last!' said Akbar, turning to his best friend. 'Go and find me this thief.'

Birbal hushed the crowd and waited. A few moments later, all were silent.

'What nonsense is this?' asked Abdul Qadir. 'What use is a donkey's tail in any test? Birbal makes fools of us all, I say!'

'SILENCE!' ordered Akbar. 'I value your advice, Abdul Qadir, but do not question Birbal. How many times must he prove his worth to you all?'

Abdul, chastened and defeated once again, slid back amongst the crowd. Birbal cleared his throat. 'I want every person, here and outside, to raise the hand with which they lifted the donkey's tail. Just that hand, wide open.'

He gestured to the guards.

'Find me the person whose fingers are not blackened.'

For Birbal had painted the underside of the donkey's tail with black paint. The thief, he'd realized, would be the one who did not lift up the donkey's tail, out of fear or guilt, or both. Very quickly, and to murmurs of shock, a courtier called Alim Khan was dragged before Akbar.

'Here he is, Your Majesty!'

Akbar ordered the man to show his fingers.

'But, Your Majesty, I . . .'

'Your hand!' said Akbar, as the guards drew their swords.

Alim Khan did as instructed and his hand was clean.

'We have our thief!' said Birbal.

As the guards dragged the guilty man away, Akbar asked Birbal what his reward should be.

'I require nothing, Your Majesty,' Birbal replied. 'But perhaps it would be wise to give Fazal something for his troubles . . .?'

Akbar smiled. 'It shall be done,' he said. 'Now, time for another riddle . . .'

TALES FROM INDIA

With Puffin Classics, the adventure isn't over when you reach the final page. Want to discover more about the people and places that inspired these stories? Read on . . .

CONTENTS

AKBAR AND FRIENDS

Did you know that the Emperor Akbar, Birbal and Abdul Qadir were real people?

Akbar (1542–1605)

The Emperor Akbar's name was Abu'l-Fath Jalal-ud-din Muhammad Akbar. Akbar means 'Great'. He is often referred to as Akbar the Great – which means 'Great the Great'!

Akbar came to the throne of the Mughal Empire in India when he was thirteen. He was a fine soldier, and conquered lands all across northern and central India. He reformed the way his empire was governed so it worked well, justly and fairly, and tolerated people of many different races and religions. Akbar was brought up as a Sunni Muslim, but during his life he tried to bring Islam, Hinduism, Zoroastrianism and Christianity closer together in a system named Din-i-llahi. This upset some members of the original religions who did not want to accept any changes.

He liked drinking water from the Ganges River, and had this water sent in sealed jars carried by teams of water-carriers to whichever part of India he was in. He enjoyed playing the game Pachisi – we know this in a simplified form as Ludo (Parcheesi in the United States). Akbar also liked eating fruit, and as he grew older, he gave up eating meat.

Akbar founded a great library with over 24,000 books in it, in many different languages. He encouraged poets, writers, scholars, musicians, craftsmen and readers to come to his court for study and discussion. Every day someone read to him, as he loved literature – but he never learned to read or write!

Birbal (1528–1586)

Birbal's real name was Mahesh Das. His nickname, 'Birbal', was given to him by Akbar – it means 'courageous and great', which was a joke. He was not particularly brave, or a skilled soldier! Birbal was a Brahmin, a member of a group of Hindus who were scholars and priests. Educated to know the Hindi, Sanskrit and Persian languages, he was a poet and musician. After his appointment to Akbar's court, Birbal soon became the 'Kavi Rai' (the poet laureate). He was the only courtier to have a house within the walls of Akbar's palace at Fatehpur Sikri

Abdul Qadir (1540–1615)

Abd al-Qadir Bada'uni was one of Akbar's court historians and translators. He was a traditional Muslim and, along with other Muslims at court, disliked Birbal because he was a Hindu. He agreed Birbal was a good musician, but thought he had too much influence over Akbar. Akbar asked Abdul to write several books for him. The most important is *Muntakhab al-tawārīkh* (*Selection from History*), often called *Tārīkh-e Badāūnī* (*Badāūnī's History*), a history of Muslim India. Abdul Qadir also translated the great Hindu epics the *Ramayana* and the *Mahabharata*.

In the stories we meet characters from two of the world's great religions – Hinduism and Islam. There are many people who belong to these two faiths in India, along with those of other faiths, including Buddhism (which started in India), Zoroastrianism, Sikhism, Christianity and Jainism. The Emperor Akbar tried to bring some of them closer together by emphasizing things that were similar, but in the end he did not succeed.

Hinduism is one of the world's oldest religions. Most Hindus live in India, though it has influenced people across the world. Unlike other religions, Hindus have many sacred books and writings. Some people study by going to an ashram, a place where religion can be taught away from the activities of the world outside.

Hindus have many gods and goddesses, but these are usually thought to be particular aspects of Brahman, a universal spirit. The most important gods who make up Brahman are Brahma, the creator of the universe, Vishnu, who preserves it, and Shiva, who destroys it.

Shiva's wife is Parvati, who appears in these stories. She is much loved, and is the goddess of motherhood. But in another form she is also Kali, the goddess of destruction. Ram (or Rama) is one of the aspects of the god Vishnu. He is the perfect man, whether considered as son, brother, teacher, husband or king.

Hindus see how time moves, from birth to death and from creation to destruction. They believe that the soul doesn't die. When a body dies, its soul is reborn. This is called 'reincarnation'. Animals are reincarnated, as well as people. If you live a good life, you will be reborn into a better state, and if you are bad, you will be born into a worse one. This is a law called karma.

There are many holidays and festivals in Hinduism. One important festival is Diwali, which falls in October or November. It is a festival of light.

Islam started in Arabia, where around AD 600, the Prophet Mohammed began to preach in Mecca. He believed he had been called to teach his people to worship Allah (God). He taught them that there was only one God, and that he was God's messenger.

Mohammed's companions wrote down his teachings and revelations and eventually they became the Muslim holy book, the Koran. Islam teaches that Allah created the whole universe, and has absolute power. He is just and merciful, but humans should behave well. They should be just and honest. They should be kind to the poor and unfortunate. Life on earth is a test, and angels in heaven keep a record of how each human behaves.

On the day of judgement, a good person will be given his record book to hold in his right hand, and he will go to heaven. A bad person will have to take their book in their left hand, and go to hell.

One special group of Muslims are the Sufis. A Sufi tries to make his worship as perfect as possible. He will reject worldly things, concentrating instead on prayer and thought and study.

Sikhism was founded in the sixteenth century by Guru Nanak, a Hindu who lived during the time of the Mughal emperor Babur. Today, there are about 20 million Sikhs worldwide. Sikhism stresses the importance of doing good deeds – living honestly, treating everyone equally and being generous to those in need – rather than rituals. Sikhs believe in one God, who is kept in the mind and heart at all times.

A challenge!
Can you think of any other religions? Can you find out some things about one you haven't come across before? If you met someone who belonged to that religion, what questions would you like to ask to find out more?

and the Taj Mahal. But his court was so luxurious it started to cost more than the money available.

Shah Jahan's son, Aurangzeb, extended the empire even more. In his day, he ruled over almost all of India, and over nearly a quarter of the world's population. However, he was not tolerant. He persecuted his Sikh and Hindu subjects, and destroyed many Hindu temples. The Mahrattas, Hindus from Central India, rose against him, and this seriously weakened the empire. After Aurangzeb's death it began to break up.

The empire finally ended when the British captured Delhi in 1858.

Write your autobiography
The person you know best is you. What things would you like other people to know about you? What have you already done in your life? What would you like to do — study something special? Help people in need? Change the world? Have a go at writing your autobiography, like Babur.

The Mughal Empire was founded by Babur, a prince of Afghanistan. When he was driven out of his kingdom of Samarkand, he invaded India in 1526, and defeated the Sultan of Delhi, taking his lands to rule. Later success in war brought him more territory.

Babur (a Persian nickname: it means 'Tiger') was not Indian. He was a mixture of Turk and Mongol. His mother was a descendant of Genghis Khan, his father was a descendant of Tamerlane, and he had been brought up in the Persian tradition. The Persian word for 'Mongol' is 'Moghul' and this gave his empire its name.

Babur wrote poems, many of which became popular folk songs, and also wrote his autobiography. He said, 'The new year, the spring, the wine and the beloved are joyful. Babur make merry, for the world will not be there for you a second time.'

Babur's grandson, Akbar, was the greatest of the Mughal emperors. Akbar came to the throne in 1556. He was a good soldier, and expanded the empire. He ruled justly and with tolerance, and people of many religions and races served him loyally.

son, Shah Jahan, loved architecture. He had buildings constructed, including the Red Fort

ANIMALS SNAKES AND LADDERS

Snakes and ladders is a very ancient board game invented in India. It's now world-famous.

In the original game, the ladders represented good qualities, such as generosity and knowledge. The snakes were bad qualities – anger, telling lies, disobedience. There were more snakes than ladders, because it's harder to be good and get to heaven than it is to be bad and slide back down to earth!

In the stories, there are many animals and birds. Some help humans, and some don't. Try making your own snakes and ladders board, using good animals on the ladders and bad animals on the snakes. Read the stories carefully, because some animals help people when you might think they wouldn't, and others are unhelpful when you might expect them to be kind.

You will need:

- A big sheet of paper
- A ruler
- Coloured pencils or felt-tips
- A dice
- Counters (use buttons or pebbles if you don't ha

THE CASTE SYSTEM

In ancient India, people were divided into groups, called castes, mostly depending on what they did. Some work was more highly thought of than others. You were born into a caste, married someone of the same caste, and couldn't leave it. Members of each group belonged to the same religious sects, and had about the same amount of wealth as other group members. The groups were known as varnas, or colours.

- Brahmins (white) were priests, teachers and scholars
- Ksatriyas (red) were nobles and warriors
- Vaishyas (yellow) were farmers, merchants, bankers and craftspeople
- Shudras (black) were servants and labourers

Over time, the groups divided and subdivided, until eventually there were more than 3,000 castes. Then another group emerged – the outcastes, or untouchables, often called dalits. They did the dirtiest kinds of jobs, like tanning skins to make leather. In 1950 India outlawed untouchability. Equal status was granted to all people. However, it has proved very difficult to do away with the system.

What do you think?

What do you think about dividing people up like this? Can you think of some good things about the system, and some bad ones?

Rule a grid with 100 squares in it – 10 squares along the bottom row, and 10 rows of 10 squares each going up. Number every square – square 10 should be the bottom right-hand corner, and square 11 is the one right above.

Work out where your good animal ladders and your bad animal snakes will go. Each one must clearly start and finish in a square. Colour them in, and decorate the outside of the paper if you like.

Play the game with at least one other person. Throw the dice, and move your counter along the board according to the number of pips on the dice. If you land on a square with the bottom of a ladder on it, go up to the top and carry on from there. If you land on a square with the top of a snake on it, go down! The winner gets to square 100 first.

RICE PUDDING

Many of these stories contain special meals, banquets and feasts. One of the most popular things to eat is rice pudding! This is easy to make – why not try it?

You will need:

- 45 g (3 tbls) small-grain (pudding) rice
- 600 ml (1 pint) milk
- (25 g butter if you use semi-skimmed or skimmed milk)
- 1 tbls sugar
- Nutmeg
- An oven-proof dish

What you do:

Please ask an adult to help you before you start cooking.

Heat the oven to a temperature of 150°C/300°F/gas mark 2

Put the rice and sugar in the dish. Pour the milk slowly over the rice and sugar. (If you are using semi-skimmed or skimmed milk, add the butter to the mixture.) Sprinkle a very small amount of nutmeg on the milk.

Put the dish in the oven, and cook for 2 hours.

Take it out carefully, wearing thick oven gloves to protect your hands, or get a grown-up to do this for you.

There is enough pudding here for four people.

Rice can be flavoured with such things as cinnamon, cardamom, saffron, rosewater and vanilla. Some people add nuts or raisins – they are all delicious.

ashram – a place, usually in a remote location, where people can retreat from the world and study the Hindu religion

azure – a bright blue colour

banyan tree – a kind of fig tree in which some branches grow towards the ground, where they root and turn into extra tree trunks

bungalow – a house with only one storey. They were first built in Bengal for Europeans living in India

charpoy – a bed with a light wooden frame strung with thin rope or webbing

cohort – originally a unit of six centuries in the Roman army, now used for a group of people who share something similar

conch shell – a large, strong sea shell with a spiral shape. Some can be blown through to make a musical note

dhoti – a piece of cloth worn as clothing by some men in India. A dhoti is tied round the waist and covers part of the legs

dosa pancake – a pancake made using flour with a mixture of rice and pulses, such as peas and beans, ground together

fakir – a religious person, usually a Muslim but sometimes a Hindu, who has given up worldly things and lives on what food kindly people provide

karma – how you have lived your life – not just the one you are living now, but the lives you have had before. The total of goodness or badness will affect your future. Karma is an important part of the Hindu and Buddhist religions

khichri – a very simple dish of rice and lentils. A richer version, including eggs and fish, is known in Britain as kedgeree

okra – the long seed pods of a tropical plant, eaten as a vegetable. Okra is sometimes called 'ladies' fingers'

papaya – the fruit of the papaya tree. A papaya looks like a thin melon. It has orange flesh and small black seeds

peepal tree – a kind of fig tree held to be sacred by Buddhists, because Buddha sat under one. Also called a bo tree

pomelo – the biggest citrus fruit. It is rather like a grapefruit, with a thick yellow skin and a sour taste

prudhan – a senior government minister in India, like a prime minister

sadhu – a wise and holy man. Sadhus live very simply

saffron – a yellow-coloured spice made from a variety of crocus. Saffron can also be used as a colour

sari – a dress worn by women in India and other Asian countries. It is a piece of cotton or silk cloth, folded and wrapped round the body to give a long skirt, a covering to the top of the body, and with one end floating free

Sufi – a Sufi is a Muslim who tries to practise his religion as perfectly as possible. Sufis spend time in study, thought and prayer and reject worldly things